# BELONG BE STRONG

# Belong Be Strong

Violet Barkley

# Preface

If society says anything, even if it's been shouted from the rooftops for generations, check it with the Bible.

For example, do young adults have to fight with parents and adults in leadership?

The United States society says that's what they do as part of growing up. But if that's true, then it should be true in other cultures as well. Is it true worldwide in every culture? No.

Young adults have choices about how to express negative emotions and experiences. So do parents.

And all ages of Christians are called by Christ to live at peace with one another, as far as it depends on each of us.

It starts with reading the Bible for yourself.

My dearest JoJo,

You know I love you. Ever since you were a baby I've held you in one arm and the Bible in the other, longing and praying for you to choose Jesus as your Savior and Lord.

I left notes for you. You know my handwriting. Pay attention. Life is bumpy, not smooth. You don't always get what you want. But God is still good.

Be gentle with Mom. She hurts, too.

I will always love you.

Most importantly, Jesus is the way. Walk with him. Compared with eternity, life doesn't last long even for someone who lives to be 100.

Stand tall. Pray for wisdom. Find your purpose and live it well. Love God with everything you've got.

Love forever,
Dad

# CONTENTS

# 1

# BELONG

When you get a word of wisdom, keep it; keep it for later.


*There's got to be more than this*, JoJo thought as another wave of unkind laughter faded and the group of girls turned the corner and walked down the gleaming high school hallway.

She felt heat flash into her cheeks during the confrontation with Amanda, the unofficial yet silently acknowledged leader of the clique. Then bewilderment set in as she wondered why they acted like cruelty was fun, especially to new students like her.

"It's not fun for everyone," JoJo mumbled to herself as she shoved a last book on top of the pile and swung her locker door closed.

"What isn't fun?" asked a boy from a few lockers down.

She turned and looked up into dark brown eyes, surprised by tenderness in them, and doubly surprised because she did not realize he was standing there.

"Oh, Hermie. Did you hear what they said?"

He nodded, and continued looking at her as if he expected an answer.

*I'm not ready to explain or to tell anyone about this*, JoJo thought, looking up at him. *I feel so embarrassed. I don't know what to do. But if I ever settle on a plan, he might be a good ally. Just not yet.*

"Maybe we can talk about it another time," she said. "I need to get to class. We have a quiz next period."

*Saved by a quiz? Perhaps far fetched*, JoJo thought, *but he seemed to accept it.*

"Okay, See you later," Herman said.

As they parted she wondered if he noticed the red in her cheeks.

*Probably not*, she thought. *but after weeks of daily embarrassment, something needs to be done about those girls.*

# 2

# COMEBACKS

What's important? Do that.

When the last bell rang for the day, JoJo opened the bottom valve on her trumpet, blew out the saliva, wiped the mouthpiece, and stashed her instrument in the case for the trip home. She hurried down the long hallway.

*Yes! The door to Mrs. Stacey's room is open!* JoJo thought, smiling. She peeked in. *And she's not tutoring reading students at the moment. Here goes.*

JoJo took a big breath then walked into the room and smiled.

As usual, Mrs. Stacey looked up with kindness and her well-known quiet smile, available for everyone.

*She will know the best thing to do,* thought JoJo, as her tale of the confrontation with the clique tumbled from her lips.

Mrs. Stacey listened, at times seemed puzzled, then perked up into a smile again.

That was not the reaction JoJo expected.

"No, JoJo," Mrs. Stacey explained. "I'm not taking sides or saying what happened was right. It's just that something very similar happened to me when I was your age. Yes, very similar."

"What did you do about it?" JoJo asked, astonished.

"First, what did you do about it?" Mrs. Stacey replied. She waited.

"At the time, I didn't know what to say. I was embarrassed," JoJo said. "Since then I've thought of about a hundred things I wish I would have said. Those comebacks always come too late."

"Would any of those things have been truly helpful?"

"I suppose not," JoJo admitted. "But at least I would not have stood there looking stupid in front of the whole group."

"Well, we have choir practice tonight, and I need to hurry home," Mrs. Stacey said. "Take a sheet of paper and write down possible responses to the situation, and what outcomes of those responses might be. What do you really want to happen, JoJo? Think it through. Let's talk about this after choir practice."

*What do I really want to happen?* JoJo thought as she headed down the hallway, out of the school building and toward home. *For weeks I've only wanted to be friends. Why does that have to be so hard?*

As JoJo walked the five blocks to her home, she thought about the put downs she endured in the most recent weeks, and stopped every now and then to scribble them and possible responses on a back page of her notebook. Some of her comebacks made her laugh out loud.

By the time she turned the large brass door knob and walked in the front door, her mood seemed lighter. At least she didn't feel so powerless against her formidable foe, Amanda.

The smell of fresh cardamom cookies sent her troubles scurrying even further.

And since her mother worked most days, seeing her when she arrived home from school made JoJo love Thursdays all the more.

# 3
# CHOICES

Listen, my heart beats for you.


JoJo found her list morphing into multiple pages by the time she finished drying the last dish and closing the cupboard door.

She and her mother talked as they worked, cleaning up after dinner.

Her mother said she understood JoJo's feelings of being rejected and pushed away.

"Sometimes relationships can be a challenge," her mother said.

"Mom, what was the worst thing you ever did as a kid?" JoJo asked.

"Funny you should ask that," her mother said. "I made a lot of mistakes as a kid, things I wish I would have done differently. I guess it's part of growing up. But probably the worst thing I ever did was treat a girl about the way those girls are treating you. I told her I didn't want to be her friend because she was too old, and she was only two grades ahead of me.

"She didn't say anything. She just turned and walked away. But I knew I hurt her feelings. I regretted it," her mother said. "I wish I would have said something, apologized. Instead, I stayed stuck in a broken relationship.

"Unkindness comes naturally. We have to learn how to treat others well. And we all need practice."

"I hadn't thought about the other girls' side of it," JoJo said. "I guess it's possible they hadn't taken any of it seriously, or hadn't considered my feelings at all. Maybe they thought it was no big deal.

"Mom, what could the other girl have done at the time to make your situation better?"

"Well, she could have chosen anger and bitterness," her mother replied. "Do you think that would have been helpful?"

"Not really, I guess. But those girls are brutal to me every day. Mom, if the girl said nothing to you, wouldn't you have done the same thing again?"

"Possibly. What responses do you have on your list?"

After reading some of them, her mother looked up and said, "JoJo, is there anything on your list other than revenge?"

"Um, not really," JoJo stammered and thought, *Mom doesn't approve.* "I want to turn it on the other girls for once, to say something to make them stop being mean and making fun of people."

"So you think being just as mean as they are is going to change them? That's not what the other girl did to me."

"She didn't?"

"No. She forgave, even though I didn't ask. Later she told me she 'walked by faith.' She didn't know what to do, either. But she prayed and trusted God. That's what strong people do when they know the Lord. And at first it isn't easy."

She glanced at the kitchen clock and reminded JoJo they needed to leave for choir practice.

*I'm confused,* JoJo thought. *I thought these were lots of great ideas. Now I just feel frustrated.*

*What really works? To forgive as if nothing happened seems too weak, and these girls didn't even bother to get to know me.*

# 4

# HEART SONGS



JoJo's mood lifted as she greeted Rosemary and Julie, and slid into her spot on the alto pew in the front of the church by the ancient upright piano.

*I love those two ladies,* JoJo thought. *They're two of the most beautiful women around, with their dark curly hair and lovely smiles. And they always seem pleasant and happy.*

Her mother sang soprano, which more suited JoJo's high voice. But since there were so few altos and JoJo could hear the harmonies from her experience in the band, she sang alto with Rosemary and Julie.

*Their strong, low voices carry the part well,* JoJo thought, as the choir worked through a song for the next Sunday.

At times she struggled to maintain support in her stomach while reaching for the lowest notes. But as they opened the book to a new song, she was quicker at sight reading music.

*We help each other,* JoJo thought. *It's okay.*

She lost herself in the music and for the whole hour never thought about her problems at school. Mrs. Stacey sat at the piano, directing the parts by sometimes singling out a section to sing alone, then at other times bringing all sections together to run through a short passage that needed strengthening.

At the end of the practice, they filed into position around a huge pipe organ in front of the sanctuary.

JoJo ran her hand along the smooth woodwork of the antique instrument and recalled when Mrs. Stacey told them a repairman said this organ was rare, and few churches kept them any more.

*I can't imagine this little country church without it,* JoJo thought. She looked up at the long brass pipes shining boldly next to the central stained glass window showing Jesus, standing at a closed door and knocking.

*That takes my breath away, always,* thought JoJo.

She watched Mrs. Stacey pull out knobs on the organ to set the sound produced by three banks of keys and foot pedals below. It seemed like the challenge of playing the old organ, somehow, pleased Mrs. Stacey.

*Or maybe it means something more,* JoJo thought, *I'm not sure.*

They practiced the choir anthem twice, then ran through the first verse of each hymn for the Sunday service.

While JoJo may have forgotten about her assignment and appointment after choir, Mrs. Stacey had not. When the others stood up and walked toward the door, Mrs. Stacey asked JoJo to sit beside her on the big organ bench.

JoJo pulled the list out of her pocket, and Mrs. Stacey reached around her small blue purse to pick up a well-worn Bible.

"JoJo," Mrs. Stacey began, "would it be okay with you if we start with something other than your list right now?"

JoJo nodded.

When I was your age, I used this Bible to decide how I should respond when things happened at school or here at church," Mrs. Stacey explained. "I was wondering. Are you willing to search God's Word for what to do in this situation at school? I'm willing to meet with you to talk, I don't know, about ideas or what you think the Word of God is saying."

She nodded again.

*The assignment seems too big,* JoJo thought. As she accepted the Bible, she almost felt panicky. But JoJo breathed deeply and opened the pages at a bookmark and read Psalm 1:

"Blessed is the man who does not walk in the counsel of the wicked or stand in the way of sinners or sit in the seat of mockers, but his delight is in the law of the Lord, and on his law he meditates day and night."

Mrs. Stacey nodded as JoJo read. It was a good starting point, she said.

"I intend to buy a Bible for you," Mrs. Stacey said, "but there was not enough time before choir practice. This can get you started on knowing how to handle problems God's' way."

*"God's way" was not something I considered for my list,* JoJo thought. *I might as well look a little further.*

JoJo thumbed through the pages, saw short notes written in the margins and words that seemed to point to a theme of a passage. In the front and back written on blank pages were prayer requests and answers with dates.

*Not to put down the teacher or anything, but this is way different from Sunday School with a short story, a memory verse and a quick prayer,* JoJo thought. *This seems more like Mrs. Stacey's way of life, and she started so long ago. The dates prove it.*

"Thank you," JoJo said, smiling. She hugged Mrs. Stacey and looked up at her mother, who also was smiling. She clutched the Bible near to her heart as they walked up the sanctuary aisle toward the big wooden double doors in the back.

# 5

# FOCUS

*Just start.*

All the way home JoJo felt hushed. It's the only way she could describe it. The feeling enveloped her when Mrs. Stacey held out her Bible and JoJo grasped it in her hands.

*In a way I felt this before,* JoJo thought, *like when I walked into the sanctuary for youth group, when no one else was there yet, I felt hushed. It's almost as if prayers from many church services lingered there, hushed.*

And young Alice's Bible, she noticed even during the quick glance at the church, seemed like a diary of sorts, of meetings with God.

That thought made her smile and reminded her of a diary she loved when she was younger. She wrote stories and drew pictures of her family and going to the beach.

*I haven't even opened my diary in a long time,* JoJo thought. *Life turned too hard, too sad for words, so I wrote none.*

JoJo refused to think more about that time in her life.

When they arrived home, JoJo reached the door first, opened it quickly and raced up the steps two at a time, her mountain climber warmup, she dubbed it.

She hung her coat on a hook behind the door to her room, tossed off her shoes on the closet floor and curled up on pillows with Alice's Bible for a few minutes, she promised herself, before finishing a North American literature book report due in the morning.

Then she felt overwhelmed again: Where do you start to read the Bible?

*Mrs. Stacey placed the bookmark at Psalm 1,* JoJo thought. *That's good enough for me.*

She read the psalm a couple of times before a realization elbowed its way into her understanding. *Wait a minute. I see a connection to my situation.*

Then in the margin she read, "God's roadblocks, my protection."

JoJo found her mother in the downstairs bathroom wrestling a plunger up and down in a sink about one quarter full of soapy water. Her face was red and she was starting to perspire from the exertion. She was out of breath.

She looked up into the mirror as JoJo walked in behind her, and they both laughed. It's what they agreed to do when they feel frustrated, to blow off steam.

"What is it, Honey?" her mother said.

"Remember when you looked at my list and said my only response was revenge?" JoJo asked.

"It seemed that way to me," her mother said.

"I wanted to be liked and accepted so bad when we came here. But nothing I ever did was good enough for these girls," JoJo said. "I was always on the wrong end of every joke. Well, Mrs. Stacey asked me to read Psalm 1. And by the third or fourth time through, I thought I could see a connection. I mean, I don't have to force this. I'm going to back up from the situation and turn my focus on God. I think that's what Mrs. Stacey meant by a note she wrote."

JoJo turned to the Psalm and showed her mother the note in the margin. The long smile on her mother's face as they looked into each others' eyes let JoJo know she understood. The other girls' rejection could be God's protection, at least for now. And at this point JoJo did not know them well enough to know for sure.

# 6
# REPORT

First work hard

JoJo did not mean to write a super short book report. After all, she did read a book by Ruth V. Ackerman all the way to the end. It's just that her secret plan needed to be ripped up and trashed in favor of a well-worn idea from an ancient book. And there wasn't much time after choir practice.

"Farm and Folly," she jotted down the title and author and thought about how she almost didn't read it because of the tragic beginning of the story. *Real life is too hard,* she thought at the time, *and I don't need more of anything negative.*

But when JoJo and her mother moved into the house in town and she changed schools, she lost internet access at home. She felt cut off from her world of friends, but her mom said she got her beautiful daughter back.

"Give me some time," her mom said. "We won't be without internet forever. It's just that moving costs so much, and it drained my bank account."

On their own, the duo made a pact to laugh off the pain when they could, and to just be there for each other when one -- or both -- needed to cry. Being held and accepted as she was at that moment meant so much to JoJo the many times her mother did that for her, she tried to give her mom the same grace when she needed it.

And lack of internet took a big dollop of grace. But she loved and admired her mother so much, treating her with respect mattered, especially now.

So out of boredom JoJo picked up the book on evenings when her mother worked late or busied herself with laundry and other chores.

*That was a good read,* JoJo thought as she finished it. *I'm glad I gave it a second chance.*

For the book report JoJo described the main character, Ginny, and compared difficulties of Ginny's life with her own.

As a personal touch, JoJo compared how Ginny fell in love and knew Jerry was "the one," for example, compared with how JoJo always felt like true love would happen.

"Boys are always around and they're cute and everything," JoJo wrote, "but there has not been a connection, that spark of...something."

And she determined even before her father's illness that true love is mutual, built on respect and honor.

Her mind wandered to favorite memories from when she was a tiny child: Her mother and father gazing into each other's eyes and working together in the kitchen with playfulness she hoped to reenact with her someone someday.

JoJo sighed, finished the closing paragraph of the book report, signed her name to the bottom and created a title page with her name and class section and the teacher's name. She opened her three-ring binder and stashed the report in the literature section, set the notebook on her books by the door and turned out the light for the night.

As thoughts slowed and dwindled into sleep, her mind swirled her concepts of true love with swiftly moving music notes, and what Alice's Bible might say about it.

# 7

# DETOUR

*Practice the art and it will not fail you.*


When JoJo walked in she saw the school building was prepped for the football game with long spirit posters painted with strings of bold letters in bright colors by the pep club and stuck to the wall with gobs of masking tape.

She knew who the varsity football players were by the dress shirts tucked into blue jeans, and neckties.

*They have no clue,* she thought, *how good they look dressed like that.*

To the right the group of girls in the clique started forming at the corner of the hallway they always chose so they could see and be seen. Some wore cheerleading uniforms. Others wore pep club t-shirts with jeans.

*It's not about cowardice,* JoJo thought as she stopped by the trophy case and pretended to be looking for someone. *Every day I walk past the group and every day I get the same humiliating treatment from them. Today will be different.*

Instead of turning to the right, JoJo turned toward the left to walk past Mrs. Stacey's room.

*A quick chat with Mrs. Stacey would be better by far than another embarrassed stammering defeat,* JoJo thought, calculating the walk in that direction would only be about 30 feet longer.

*It's worth it,* JoJo thought. *I need to try something different if I want different results.*

Several small children milled about in Mrs. Stacey's room, choosing a book from a shelf or caring for the class rabbit, Mr. Wiggley.

"Good morning," JoJo called as she stopped at the doorway. "How are you today?"

"I'm ready for the best day ever," Mrs. Stacey said, grinning. "How about you?"

"Same," JoJo said, and she laughed. *Really, I'm hoping for survival. Optimism feels strange. But why not try for the best day ever instead?* JoJo thought.

"I was thinking about Psalm 1, and the note in the margin," JoJo said. "Maybe my not being accepted by the other girls might be God's protection?"

"Perhaps," Mrs. Stacey replied. "God does work in our circumstances. And when we ask Him, he guides us."

"I'm not really sure how to pray about this," JoJo said.

"Prayer is talking to God, like you're talking to me," Mrs. Stacey said. "Be honest, ask for God's help, and thank him."

"Thank you," JoJo said as she hugged Mrs. Stacey, then hurried down the hallway. If she went to the instrument storage area, she probably could pray quickly before class.

*Yes! No one is around,* JoJo thought as she stood by her trumpet case, bowed her head and closed her eyes.

"Dear God, you know all the trouble I'm having with the girls. I don't know what to do. So I'm asking you to show me and help me. Thank you in advance. In Jesus' name, amen," she said.

With just enough time to get to class, JoJo rounded the corner quickly and hurried to her locker. The girls were staring at her, not saying a word.

*That's unusual,* JoJo thought.

She twirled her combination on the lock and yanked open the door. Just then books and notebooks tumbled from the locker and slammed into her arms, stomach and legs, and she dropped the notebooks and books she was holding. All this was accompanied by gleeful laughter from the girls.

*Being hit by the books hurt, but not as much as the unkindness,* JoJo thought. She blinked back tears and sighed to regain composure before bending to pick up everything.

*No one ever stacked my locker before,* JoJo thought, *and I've never done it to anyone, either.*

In a grandiose mocking show, Amanda trotted up to her and said in a false voice, "Oh, poor JoJo! Here, let me help you."

Angry, JoJo looked into Amanda's eyes for a few moments as they both picked up books and notebooks, and JoJo placed her items in the locker and chose the ones she needed for the next class.

She resisted an overwhelming urge to scream at the girl, and instead mumbled, "Thank you."

*It's hard to forgive when you're hurting,* JoJo thought, as she plopped down in her desk. She wondered if the burning red scrapes on her arms would turn to bruises.

Behind her and a few rows over, Amanda scribbled quickly on a sheet of paper.

*What is that,* JoJo thought, *her list of humiliating accomplishments?*

Other students walked to the front of the room and dropped their book reports on the right corner of Mrs.

Smith's desk. Amanda joined them. But as JoJo rubbed her sore arm and opened her North American literature notebook, her book report was gone.

She felt her heart in her throat. She frantically flipped through pages and pages of the notebook, but not only was the report not where JoJo placed it the night before, it wasn't in her notebook at all.

*God, don't let me cry in front of the class. God, don't let me cry in front of the class,* JoJo begged. She could feel her face heating up. *I always turn in my homework on time.* She fanned her face with her notebook and closed her eyes for a few moments. She did not see Mrs. Smith walk up to her, but felt a gentle hand on her shoulder.

"JoJo, are you feeling okay?" Mrs. Smith asked kindly.

JoJo opened her eyes and looked up at Mrs. Smith with a smile -- like she and her mother often do with each other -- and asked if they could talk after class. Mrs. Smith nodded, smiled back and walked to the front as she instructed the class to open their books to page 47.

*How did that happen?* JoJo asked herself. *The pressure of the panic lifted when Mrs. Smith placed her hand on my shoulder.*

Still, the whole period JoJo had to refocus her mind on the lesson over and over. She felt weak, like all of the energy drained out of her, and the day was just beginning.

At the end of the class, JoJo walked up to where Mrs. Smith sorted papers at her desk.

"I know you get empty excuses about homework all the time," JoJo said, "but I really did do my book report for today. Then when I looked for it, it wasn't in my notebook where I put it last night."

Mrs. Smith looked up from the papers.

"What was the book?" she asked.

"Farm and Folly," JoJo answered.

"And the author?"

"Ruth V. Ackerman."

What was the story about? Mrs. Smith asked.

JoJo described her reluctance at first to read the book because of the tragic beginning, and then told Mrs. Smith about her comparisons between the book and her parents' keeping romance alive in their relationship. It was more than letting it happen, she explained.

"Okay," Mrs. Smith said. "You convinced me. If you will write the book report for me and have it on my desk on Monday, I will give you credit. And by the way, I saw what happened this morning. Are you really okay?"

"I think so," JoJo said. "Your kindness really helped. Now I understand why Mom says sometimes a simple gesture of kindness can make all the difference. It really did for me today. So thank you."

When JoJo rushed to her locker to collect her book and notebook for algebra class, Herman stood at his locker, too.

"Ha, ha. Saw what happened. That was classic," Herman said.

"Oh, Hermie. You saw?" JoJo said, wishing he would just go to class. She didn't have time to talk.

"Ha, ha. Yeah. Saw them doing it. That was classic, too."

"And you didn't stop them or warn me? Why not?" JoJo glared at him.

"What's the fun in that?" he asked, grinning.

"If it's not fun for everyone, it's not fun," JoJo said, annoyed and wanting to end the conversation. She opened her locker slowly; the books stayed. She grabbed the algebra to rush to class, but stopped beside Herman.

"Wait a minute. How did they get my locker combination?"

Herman looked at the ceiling, then at JoJo, "One of the girls works in the office fourth period."

# 8
# FIELD STUDY

*You will know them by their deeds.*


JoJo could only hope her answers were correct on the algebra quiz.

Normally, a quiz is only a brief review of homework and a few days of class instruction. But today JoJo found it difficult to focus on anything, let alone algebra.

*God, help!* she prayed silently. She sighed and methodically worked each problem. But her heart wasn't in it.

*If I still have a heart at all,* she thought, *because I can't feel it.*

As she turned in the quiz she realized she forgot to sign her name.

*That would have been a big fat zero,* she thought, as she scribbled her name on the top and handed it in.

She followed the others out of the room and looped into the biology room, hoping the soured mood would improve.

*After all,* she thought, *I'm a Christian. I'm supposed to have the joy of the Lord... So where is the joy? But what do you do on days like today when it seems like you've fallen beneath an avalanche?*

*I just can't move my mood,* JoJo thought.

*At least in biology the quiz was earlier in the week,* she thought. *That peels off part of the usual Friday morning stress load.*

JoJo opened the textbook to Chapter 4 and gazed at large photographs of insects.

*I had no idea,* JoJo thought as she flipped the pages. *And God made all this. Where did he come up with it?*

While curiosity led her deeper into the worlds of other species, she was not prepared for the lab assignment: Go catch grasshoppers.

*Um, what? Just how do you do that?* JoJo asked herself.

The class divided into partners equipped with butterfly nets, jars with lids, notebooks and pencils.

JoJo's partner was Sharon, a quiet girl with very long brown hair and glasses.

*We share a lot of classes,* JoJo thought, *but we've never spoken to each other.*

"Have you ever caught a grasshopper before?" JoJo asked.

"No, have you?" Sharon countered.

"No. It looks like we're at a disadvantage here."

JoJo was sure the boys had grabbed a few insects in their day. She thought the creatures were interesting to look at, but she did not want one crawling on her. she found the teacher.

"Mr. Markel, how do you catch a grasshopper?" JoJo asked.

Usually fairly somber, his expression brightened with the question.

"Look for a big one. There are lots of them at this time of the year. Put the net down over it, and when it jumps into the net, it's easier to grab it and hold it. Then bring the jar and lid under the net, drop the grasshopper in and close the lid. It's easy. Just try not to squish it," he said.

JoJo noticed a twinkle in his eyes.

"Are you a science teacher because you love catching bugs?" JoJo asked.

"Insects. And, yes. I love catching insects. They're fascinating. You better get started," he said.

JoJo turned to Sharon, "Do you want the net or the jar?"

"You choose," Sharon said.

"Okay, I'm net, you're jar."

JoJo chose an area with fewer students around, crouched low to the ground and looked for grasshoppers. But it seemed like when she found one, it hopped as she was moving the net around to get it. Sharon watched for some time.

"That's not how the boys are doing it," Sharon said.

"Okay, you do the net," JoJo said, handing it to her in exchange for the jar and lid.

"I've done this with butterflies, not grasshoppers," Sharon said. "I don't like grasshoppers. Their feet grab you when they get on you."

"Ewww," JoJo said. She watched Sharon hold the net up and slowly walk in the grass, then pounce.

"It's a big one!" they both shouted.

The grasshopper lunged powerfully up into the net and wriggled as Sharon grabbed it by the back and held it. JoJo slid the jar and lid underneath the edge of the net and up to the grasshopper, but since its leg was stuck in the net, the girls had to work with it to gt it in the jar.

"Finally!"

With triumphant smiles they showed their specimen to Mr. Markel and followed the rest of the class into the biology lab.

"Good work with the net," JoJo said.

"Thanks," said Sharon. "We're a team."

"Okay, class," Mr. Markel spoke loudly and waited for the chatter to hush. "I heard a lot of questions out in the field, though not necessarily directed to me. I'm going to answer them, anyway.

"Number 1: Why grasshoppers? As you looked around outside, how many grasshoppers did you see? Lots of them! That's one reason. Also, have any of you compared your grasshoppers with the photographs in your textbooks? Yes, there are many different varieties, different ages. Also, they're really cool to look at up close.

"There's one more reason," Mr. Markel said. He paused. "Has anyone heard what the weather is supposed to be like this weekend? Yes, it's supposed to get cold at night. We're supposed to get a heavy frost. If it's a killing frost, these grasshoppers and many other insects are going to die, anyway. We might as well learn from them while they're available to us."

As the lab period ended, the students placed masking tape on the jars with their names and lab period, and poked blades of grass into the holes in the lids.

"These grasshoppers probably will not survive until Monday," Mr. Markel said. "Just warning you."

As they left the room together, JoJo turned to Sharon.

"Thank you for being my partner," JoJo said. "How long have you gone to this school?"

"I'm new this year," Sharon said.

"Really? I'm new, too," JoJo said.

"I've seen you," Sharon said. "I usually sit in the back so I see a lot. Why are those girls always on your case?"

"I don't know, honestly," JoJo said. "I said, 'Hi,' to them, trying to make friends, and they have been mean ever since. It wasn't like that at my old school. We all tried to be friends with everybody."

"My old school was worse. Nobody dared talk to any-body. You could get beat up," Sharon said. "I knew Amanda from there. She came here last year. So when I saw her here, I kept my distance."

"Well, I'm not like that," JoJo said. "Do you have lunch this period?"

"As a matter of fact, yes," Sharon said.

"Do you want to sit with me?" JoJo asked.

"Yes. That's a good idea," Sharon said.

And to JoJo's surprise, Sharon's locker was just on the other side of Herman's.

*Why didn't I notice that before?* JoJo thought. *It might have saved tons of heartache.*

# 9
# EXTRA EFFORT

Struggle along the way, but finish strong.

JoJo learned a few years earlier she needed to work extra hard at any subject having to do with history. It never came naturally to her.

Then this year the teachers teamed up by having the students study North American literature at the same time as North American history.

*That's double the trouble,* JoJo thought. While she could understand the events in history, the bigger picture, she struggled to remember names and dates when they were strung along like disconnected facts. But the fuller stories of the people who made history captured her imagination with their struggles and emotions.

And the good thing about Mrs. Henry, the teacher, was she seemed to understand. She reconnected everything with stories that tied the people together.

Still, JoJo had to compensate for her lack of recalling facts with extra work.

As Mrs. Henry talked, JoJo scribbled notes furiously with page references in the text so she could go back later and double check spellings and dates.

Also, JoJo found if she spent 15 or 20 minutes a day re-copying her notes and writing down dates and events three times, then her scores improved by a letter grade, easily.

After handing in her chapter quiz on the beginnings of migration from the East Coast to the Appalachian Mountains, JoJo thumbed through the next chapter in the book, "The Appalachian Trail," while others stared out of the window or passed notes under desks.

*I need a head start,* JoJo thought, kicking her self-motivated discipline into action. She read captions under photographs, browsed the chapter headings, and most importantly, read the questions at the back of the chapter. That habit she learned from Mrs. Stacey, who told her she reads those questions for review as she prepares to teach a new chapter.

"It's like priming a pump," Mrs. Stacey said with a knowing nod.

"What do you mean?" JoJo asked.

"When they drill a water well and install a new pump," Mrs. Stacey told her, "they pour some water down the pump to help it get started. That's called priming a pump. So to me, preparing for a new chapter is like priming a pump."

# 10

# LET'S DO LUNCH

When you can't find a way, say a prayer, sing a song.

Nothing was a surprise in JoJo's lunch since she packed it herself. But the cinnamon and brown sugar on her peanut butter sandwich tasted all the more sweet with someone to share a spot with her. She munched quietly, as did Sharon after she plopped her school lunch tray on the table and dug into the chicken fajitas.

With the sandwich accomplished, JoJo spoke as she opened a plastic bag containing her cookies.

"Would you like a cardamom cookie?" JoJo asked. "I'm willing to share what I consider one of the best cookies ever created. My mom and I crave cardamom cookies. And having them is a treat."

"What is that?" Sharon asked, adding she had never heard of it.

"Cardamom is a spice used in Scandinavia," JoJo explained. "Mom found the recipe in a Christmas cookbook."

"How about if I try just a little bit?" Sharon asked.

JoJo broke one of the round, flat cookies in half and handed it to Sharon, who sniffed it then took a bite.

"It's really different, isn't it?" JoJo asked, smiling.

"Different, but in a good way," Sharon said.

*At least we have cardamom cookies in common,* JoJo thought, *and grasshoppers.*

"What types of things do you like to do?" JoJo asked.

"Draw, paint," Sharon said. "Lately I've been getting into that."

"Oh," JoJo said. "I can't draw."

"I used to say that, too," Sharon offered. "But mom made me go to art therapy this summer. That changed every-thing."

"Therapy so you can do art?" asked JoJo.

"No, not really," Sharon said. "Instead of painting things, you paint feelings in art therapy."

The idea interested JoJo, but they needed to scramble to throw out their trash from lunch and head to class.

*The lunch period is always too short,* JoJo thought. *I still don't know much about Sharon. At least she likes cardamom cookies.*

# 11

# STRUGGLE

Bless and be a blessing.

As JoJo checked off the classes in her planner, she felt twinges of pain increasing from the bruises on her arm and stomach reminding her of the morning meanness. But emotionally, the effects of the prank seemed to reach down inside her somehow as the day wore on. She struggled to keep her chin up and smile. Meanwhile, inside she felt like, like nothing.

And she didn't want to go near her locker. She made herself go there and exchange books and notebooks, warily opening the door. Sadness filled the space since a general feeling of safety was gone.

*I don't feel safe,* JoJo thought, *not at school, not anymore.*

It felt like when her dad went to the hospital the last time before hospice. The other times she and her mother visited at the hospital with hope and encouragement and love.

But the last time, the love was still there, and so was sadness and heartache. No words.

JoJo closed the locker door and turned up the hall to go to 7th period study hall.

*It was just a prank,* she thought. She shook her head against tears, like she always did, and walked into the large open room to find her spot for digging out from under the end-of-the-week homework pile. *It was no big deal. It was just a prank, no biggie, no biggie deal.*

# 12

# INTO THE WELL

"A stitch in time saves nine."

Seventh period study hall filled quickly with the usual jostling and joking around of groups of friends until the monitor called out loudly, "Find your seats."

JoJo felt thankful for the hush.

She opened the planner and scanned the assignments for next week, hoping to knock off several and plan when to do the others. It was her way of easing school stress.

*I have a plan,* JoJo thought, *the worry can take a hike.*

She reread the algebra section, then looked over the example problems. She set up the page.

*Focus on one problem at a time,* she thought, *only one at a time. I can do this.*

But she just sat there.

"What is wrong with me?" JoJo said under her breath, not even a whisper.

She tried to focus on the first math problem again, but her mind just seemed blank. She saw the problem written on the page, but no calculations followed. She sighed.

*I don't know what to do,* JoJo thought. *I don't know how to do this. Why don't I know how to do this?*

A helpless feeling surged upward, and she felt as if it were choking her as she blinked away tears and fought a pulsing feeling of panic.

*Wait,* JoJo thought, *let it go. I can just let it go.*

She breathed deeply, and exhaled slowly. Eventually a sort of calm returned, but a feeling of blank numbness remained.

*I need a break,* JoJo thought, *a break from meanness.*

She sat there.

*The pain from the bruises is not really that* bad, she thought, *but it keeps nagging at me when I least want to notice it. Why can't I do this math problem?*

She reread the algebra section again, hoping something would stick. It just seemed to be flowing through her eyes into her brain and out again quickly, oh so quickly.

"God, help!" JoJo prayed quietly. Her words were lost in the rising din of the study hall, only heard by the One intended.

Unable to concentrate, she accomplished little that period.

*I give up,* JoJo thought. *I feel so helpless. Nothing works. I can't break out of this.*

She gathered her books as the clock slowly closed the period. She waited for the surge of students to push through the door before following after, wanting to avoid the crush of the rush.

*Band is next,* she thought, *a welcome distraction on a day like today.*

# 13

# UNITY

One small part of a whole.


"Quick time, one-two, one-two, one-two..."

The band director stood before the more than 100 students with a presence JoJo couldn't quite describe.

While Mr. McCluggage was demanding and challenging of all of the students, his forcefulness in commanding instruments into a well-blended whole held an extra dimension.

JoJo always -- always -- wanted to play her best for him.

And from the very first day of summer practices, he set an expectation of oneness in the group. It didn't matter what happened in math class or gym class or after school or on weekends, he said. "When the band is together, we are one."

And he proved he was there for them when someone was entering the storage room and breaking instruments. He acted quickly. The pranksters were stopped and instruments were repaired within days.

Trying to figure out what it was about Mr. McCluggage, JoJo watched him.

*Even when no one is talking and the band is not playing, Mr. McCluggage always seems to be listening,* JoJo thought. *He tilts his head slightly and then starts beating time with his baton. His hands raise and the next song begins!*

JoJo loved this next song. It featured trumpets breaking into a chord, each section at a different time in the measure with no margin for sloppiness or error. Everything had to be precise to carry this tune, Mr. McCluggage told them.

JoJo played first chair second part for marching band, which actually meant she earned third chair in the entire trumpet section. The first two played first part, JoJo provided leadership on the second part, and Bobby, on third part.

Regardless of chair, each member worked hard to be "worthy of the band and the music," as Mr. McCluggage said to them often.

On that first day of band camp in August when he pointed JoJo to her chair, she felt grateful her parents started her with private lessons and continued them while her father was sick. Now, the hours of practice were paying off in her enjoyment of band.

"Time is short," Mr. McCluggage said. "We perform for a pep assembly in 20 minutes. This is the venue to break out this fabulous song for a captive audience."

He grinned and chuckled. They practiced the beginning twice, quickly, then ran through the entire song.

"At the assembly," Mr. McCluggage said, "trumpets will be called to the front to stand, feet slightly apart, two feet behind the sideline on the basketball court, two feet. Then turn your heads slightly to the left to look at me. I'm the glue. This song needs lots of glue. Don't neglect the glue."

# 14
# MARCH

*Kindness always returns to you, usually disguised.*

"We're ready!" JoJo exclaimed with a grin. Her section mates smiled at her.

Since the band room perched on the west end of the building farthest from the gymnasium, Mr. McCluggage gave the order for lining up in sections as the rest of the student body filed into the expansive gymnasium.

The parade formation featured trombones in front, followed by explosive drum cadences echoed by calls from the rest of the band, so everyone in the whole school knew when they were coming.

"And they better hustle out of the way," Mr. McCluggage said.

JoJo felt a rush of confidence and expectation of a great pep assembly performance as she looked at facial expressions of band members near her.

*They feel it, too,* JoJo thought.

All through the long hall the cadences reverberated until the first of the band entered the gym and rounded the corner onto the basketball court.

JoJo was looking at her second trumpet section and was giving her call as they turned the corner at the edge of the bleachers. Just then a foot hooked her left leg at the ankle and she involuntarily shrieked as she sprawled to the floor. Her trumpet was kicked by the band member in front of her, and she landed on her left elbow and side, while trying to protect the instrument. Sharp surging pains bolted up her arm and into her shoulder.

A couple of band members tripped on her, but managed to keep going. Some band members quickly swerved to avoid a pileup. Then she heard the oompah of a tuba player finishing the cadence behind her, when he should have been up by the rest of his section in the formation.

Everyone was looking at JoJo.

She looked up at the tuba player and said a weak, "Thank you." She didn't even know his name, yet he stopped others from stomping on her. He nodded and joined the rest of the band.

*I'm so embarrassed,* JoJo thought, *I feel shaky.*

The gym teacher and Mr. McCluggage rushed to her.

"JoJo, are you okay?" asked Mr. McCluggage as he knelt by her.

"I, I think so," JoJo said, but she couldn't get up right away.

"I've got this," the gym teacher said. He sent an aide for several ice packs and called football players to line up between JoJo and the student body, shoulder to shoulder like a wall.

Mr. McCluggage roused the band into the school fight song, then called the trumpets forward. By then, JoJo was sitting on the floor while they applied the ice on her elbow and legs where she had been stepped on. She hid her face in one hand.

*I'm mad. I'm in pain,* JoJo thought, *but my band sounds so good.*

"Do you think you can walk?" the gym teacher asked gently.

"I'll try," JoJo said. He and the aide helped her up and they moved slowly to the office to avoid the end-of-assembly student stampede.

*At least I didn't have to be carried,* JoJo thought. *Must be a good sign.*

But her hand and arm started going numb, she hurt all over, and she didn't know what to do next.

# 15

# NOW WHAT

There is a way; walk through it.

*I'm so thankful for the nurse's office,* JoJo thought as the teacher helped her sit down on the vinyl-covered cot in relative quiet. Outside the door students laughed, talked and jostled noisily in the hallway. They were heading home.

"Is Mrs. Alice Stacey still here?" JoJo asked. Her mind raced for options, even for getting home from school. She did not think she could walk the whole way. And the pain in her left arm seemed to be surging.

"Do you want us to call your mother?" the gym teacher asked.

"She isn't home yet," JoJo said. "She's at work, but she might be getting off in a little while. She plans to go to the game."

*Oh, the game,* JoJo thought, and just then Mr. McCluggage arrived at the doorway.

"Mr. McCluggage! I'm so sorry!" JoJo exclaimed.

"What are you sorry for?" the teachers said in unison.

"It was an accident, JoJo. You didn't do anything wrong," Mr. McCluggage said gently. "How are you doing?"

"It hurts," JoJo said, "and my hand and arm are going numb. I can hardly move. But it's not my playing hand."

She looked up at him and smiled, weakly but hopefully.

A couple of band members walked into the office.

"Sorry," one said. "Are you okay? I didn't mean to step on you."

"Yeah, I didn't mean to, either," the other offered.

"I know, guys," JoJo said. "It couldn't have been helped."

"Say, Terry," the gym teacher said. "You've attended here a while. Do you know Mrs. Stacey?"

"Sure," he said.

"Would you please go to her room and see if she could come up here? JoJo asked for her," the gym teacher said.

"Yup," Terry said, and hustled down the hallway.

"JoJo, this is a call your mom needs to make, but I think you should go to the doctor to get checked out," Mr. McCluggage said.

"Maybe if I can get in right away, I can still make the game tonight," JoJo said. Her mind churning with everything she would need to do to return to the school before the 6 p.m. uniform call. It wouldn't be easy.

He smiled gently, "The most important thing is to make sure you're okay."

He scribbled a number on a piece of scrap paper.

"This is my cell phone number," he said. "As soon as you know, have your mom give me a call."

"But I don't want to be in trouble for missing a game," she countered.

"JoJo, you're not in trouble," Mr. McCluggage assured her. Just then Alice Stacey walked into the nurse's office.

"Hello," she said. "JoJo, what happened?"

"I tripped on someone's foot and fell and got stepped on," JoJo said. offering a weak smile. "Mom's at work, and I don't think I can walk home and carry everything. My arm really hurts. May I please have a ride home?"

"Do you need to go home or to the hospital?" Mrs. Stacey asked.

"I don't know," JoJo said. "Mom should get off work in a little while. I was just trying to get home first, decide later."

"I'll call her," Mrs. Stacey said, leaving the room for better cell reception at an entrance.

"You really need to be checked out," the gym teacher said. "For now, the ice is keeping down some of the swelling. But you need to find out if your arm is broken. That was a hard fall."

"You're not in trouble," Mr. McCluggage said. "I saw what happened."

"So did I," the gym teacher said, "and I know who it was."

# 16

## SCALING

Carve a big problem into smaller pieces.


"I shall do both," Alice said after her phone conversation with JoJo's mother. "I will drive you home, along with your books and things. Then we're going to the doctor. Your mother will meet us there."

JoJo listened as she cuddled her trumpet in her right arm.

"Mr. McCluggage," she said. "someone kicked it."

He held out both hands and accepted the trumpet, then inspected the bell and fluttered the valves.

"There's a small dent," he said, "but the valves work well."

He handed it back to JoJo, but held the weight of the instrument. "Play a note."

She lifted her right hand to the instrument and blew into the mouthpiece.

"Sounds fine," he said. "Quick scale."

JoJo ripped up the chromatic scale almost two octaves.

He nodded, and smiled his approval.

"You get that left arm looked at and taken care of," Mr. McCluggage said. "You're not in trouble with me, JoJo. Just let me know what the doc says. You have a place in this band any time you want it."

# 17

# WHEELS

*But tell me, what can you do?*

In spite of the ice packs, JoJo felt sore and stiff as she tried to stand up. She waited a moment, then took a few steps on her own.

"That's encouraging," the gym teacher said. "How's the arm doing now?"

"It hurts," JoJo said. "My hand...It feels really weird."

"It is swelling," the gym teacher said. "Look, you can see next to your other hand."

*He's right,* JoJo thought. She sighed.

'I need to go to my locker," JoJo said, while looking at Alice. "And I need to put my trumpet in the case."

"Would you like a ride?" the gym teacher said, unfolding a wheelchair.

JoJo looked at him and said, "You have got to be kidding me."

"Come on. Everybody is gone," he said, locking the wheels. "By the time Alice gets her things to her car, we can be ready to go, too."

*He has no idea how many times I saw my dad balk at the request of nurses that he ride in a wheelchair at the hospi-*

tal, JoJo thought. *But they wouldn't let him walk. And they were tough.*

"Get in," he urged.

"Okay," JoJo said reluctantly. She looked around to check for other students. *The school seems mostly empty,* JoJo thought. *I hurt so much! I really don't want to walk all the way to my locker. It seems so far as sore as I am, and it's only 30 feet away! I definitely don't think I can make it all the way to the band room. Plus my books and coat are there.*

"Thank you," she said, reluctantly. She turned around and sat carefully on the vinyl seat. The teacher unlocked the wheels of the chair and they headed down the hall.

JoJo blinked back tears again as he pushed her past the classrooms and lockers. Even teachers were gone. It was, after all, Friday.

*I'm truly thankful for that,* JoJo thought. *What a day already and it's not even done.*

# 18

# SMALL WORLD

Look away, look away from the pain.

The gym teacher wheeled JoJo into the instrument storage area and set the brakes on the wheelchair. JoJo slowly stood up, placed the trumpet in the crook of her left arm and opened the case with her right hand. She placed the trumpet inside and fastened the case closed.

*I don't know what to do,* JoJo thought, as she stood there looking at her stack of books and notebooks, the case and her coat.

"Here," the gym teacher said. "You sit down. I'll carry the trumpet case. You are taking it home, right?"

She nodded.

"You sit down. I'll hand your other things to you."

"Thank you so much!" JoJo said.

*This feels like being cared for,* JoJo thought, *in a kind way.*

She leaned forward as the teacher placed her coat around her shoulders. She snapped the top snap to keep it on and reached from underneath to grab the books with her right arm and snuggle them close. He unlocked the wheels, picked up the trumpet case and pushed JoJo back up the hall and outside to a staff parking area.

Mrs. Stacey was leaning into her sky blue sedan when they met her there.

"Special delivery," he said.

"Oh, thank you, George," Mrs. Staey said, smiling at him. She opened the passenger side rear door and placed the trumpet on the floor and JoJo's books on the seat.

"I don't know if I can do this," JoJo said to herself as she slowly stood up. *I'm okay,* she thought.

Mrs. Stacey closed the rear door and held open the front passenger door, waiting for JoJo.

"Thank you both so much," JoJo said as she sat in the sedan, swung her legs in, ensured her coat was around her and reached for the safety belt. She snapped it into place with her right hand, and Alice closed the door.

Even though the windows were closed, JoJo could hear part of their brief conversation.

"Thank you for your help, George. Her mother is meeting us at the doctor's office, and she already called ahead so they are waiting for us. You remember Belinda, don't you? Belinda Ward?"

"Really? I had no idea. She does resemble Belinda, come to think of it," he said. "Well, hope everything checks out okay. And thanks for your part in this, too. Be blessed."

As Alice sat down in the driver's seat, she turned toward JoJo.

"How are you doing, Sweetheart?" Alice asked.

JoJo shrugged, "As good as could be expected?"

"Okay. Your mom asked that I take you right to your doctor's office. We can get your things home later."

Alice started the car, waited for it to warm up a little bit, then pulled out of the parking lot onto the road.

JoJo watched the trees as she and Alice passed by, some of them early to change into autumn colors, but most of them green still.

"That teacher knows Mom?" she asked.

"Yes, from long ago," Alice said. "We grew up together."

# 19

# DO TELL

When fishing, you have to wait patiently...or not when they're biting.

As Alice pulled the sedan into Dr. Ken Heim's office parking lot, JoJo noticed the hospital almost directly across the street.

*How convenient,* JoJo thought. *Everything is close together in case I need X-rays.*

The digital clock on the dashboard read 3:07 p.m. as they exited the sedan and walked up to the office.

*If everything goes right,* JoJo thought, *I might make it to the game on time.*

JoJo and Alice walked up to the nurses' window and were told, "As soon as Belinda gets here, Dr. Heim wants to see JoJo right away."

Just then, JoJo's mother walked in the door.

"Alice, thank you so much! How are you doing, Babe?" her mother asked, as Alice sat down in the waiting room.

The nurse opened a door leading to the examining rooms, and they followed her to the third room on the right. She measured JoJo's height, asked her to stand on a scale, took a blood pressure reading on her right arm, handed her a blue cotton gown, asked her to change into it and left the room.

*This is embarrassing,* JoJo thought, *changing in this place. And I don't like this gown. How does it go?*

She fumbled with the clothing, but managed to change. She sat on the examining table.

*It's so cold in here,* JoJo thought. *Look at the goose bumps on my arms. And look at my swollen hand.*

She tried to move her fingers just a little.

When the nurse returned, she opened a manilla file folder and asked JoJo what happened.

"Well, the band was marching into the gym, and I tripped and fell and got stepped on," JoJo explained.

The nurse wrote on the top paper in the file.

"What hurts?" the nurse asked.

"I landed on my left arm and side. My arm hurts the most. I can't really feel my hand much. I know it's there, but it's weird. And where they stepped on me, I'm sore. They didn't mean it."

The nurse wrote some more.

*I feel awkward,* JoJo thought, *sitting on an examining table in a blue gown answering questions. I feel like crying. No. Be brave.*

She sat up straighter, and let out a long breath.

*Just be calm. Just get through this,* she thought, fighting an urge to tell the rest of the story about the books and the mean girls and the feeling like, like nothing. *Let's just take care of this and get to the game,* JoJo told herself.

Plus, she hadn't had a chance to talk it over with her mom first. *No, let's just get through this part,* she thought.

"May I see your arm that you fell on?" the nurse asked. "Can you stretch it out?"

JoJo had been afraid to try to stretch her arm out, because of the sharp pain that shot up her arm when she fell. But she did her best to hold it out and straighten it. She could nee, now, that her hand was very swollen.

"I was trying to hold up my trumpet," JoJo said, turning to her mother. "Mom, my trumpet got a dent."

"We can get another trumpet, but we can't get another you," the nurse said, smiling kindly. "But what is this?"

The nurse pointed to bruises starting to change from red to purple on the top of JoJo's arm.

"Um, they stacked my locker," JoJo said. "That's where the books fell on me."

"Was that today?" the nurse asked.

"Yes, this morning," JoJo said, solemnly.

"JoJo," her mother broke in. "Was that done by the girls you told me about?"

"They laughed," JoJo said. "But I don't know who exactly stacked my locker."

"I see," her mother said. "I'm sorry that happened to you, too."

"You've had a rough day. The doctor will be with you shortly," the nurse said. She smiled at JoJo, placed the file in the door and walked out.

*There,* JoJo thought. *I told anyway, and the telling wasn't as bad as I thought.*

# 20
# REALITY CHECK

*Big picture? It's the little things that make it.*


Briskly Dr. Ken Heim walked into the room.

*Like he always does,* JoJo thought. *But this time it really matters so I can get to the game.*

He scanned the file quickly then turned his attention to the teen seated on the examining table.

"Rough day?" he asked, his eyes inquisitive under black-rimmed eye glasses, raised bushy eyebrows and a thick mop of graying hair.

"Yes," JoJo said. "Far too much so."

He also asked her to stretch out her arm. He moved her fingers gently and felt the back of her elbow.

JoJo clenched her teeth and closed her eyes against the pain.

"That hurt?" he asked, tenderly.

"Yes," she said, eyes still closed.

*No tears, no tears,* JoJo thought.

"Mrs. Ward, I'm afraid we're going to need some X-rays on this arm and hand," Dr. Heim said. "I will write the order and call ahead to the office so they are ready when you arrive. It's getting late in the day, so please go straight over."

"We will," JoJo's mother said.

"But can I still march in the game tonight?" JoJo asked.

"Oh," the doctor said as he turned to her. "I understand...You play trumpet? I play trumpet, too. Do you think you can hold your trumpet and march and play right now?"

He waited.

The thought hit JoJo suddenly like a balloon that pops, because until that moment she was trying her best to be there for her band.

"Um, no sir," she said quietly, and looked down.

"JoJo," her mother said consolingly, "let's get you taken care of first. It will be okay. We'll work things out. We always do."

JoJo looked into her mother's eyes.

*I know she's right,* JoJo thought, but *I wasn't ready to give up hope.*

# 21

# HEART HUGS

*Keep a penny in your pocket and you're never broke.*

Undressing in the doctor's office was much easier than dressing again. JoJo gave up and asked her mother for help with simple things like buttons and zippers.

"You would do the same for me, right?" her mother said. They looked into each other's eyes for a long moment, and both laughed.

*The soreness is still here,* JoJo thought, *but I feel much better.*

When they went outside, Alice and her mother placed JoJo's school things in her mother's car; the two women hugged and parted.

"Thank you so much for helping us," Belinda said. "You made all the difference."

"I'm praying for you both," Alice said.

*I know that's true,* JoJo thought. *I saw Alice's head was bowed when we walked back into the waiting room.*

"Thank you!" JoJo called to her.

As her mother started the car she turned to JoJo. "You know, Honey, we both love you. But we don't know if we can hug you without hurting you."

"I don't know, either," JoJo said. "I'm sore all over."

Glancing at the address Dr. Heim wrote down, Belinda said casually, "This is all the way across town during rush hour."

"Then, Mom, could you please call Mr. McCluggage?" JoJo asked. "He needs to know I can't make it to the game."

"Yes, Darling. Remind me when we get to the next office." she said as she pulled the car onto the street.

# 22

# DAD'S TRICK

Faithful forever.

*Mom is handling the traffic by not handling it,* JoJo thought as Belinda turned off the main road leading to the radiologist's office for the X-ray. They were moving along on a street parallel to the main road, but several streets over. The other traffic was stopped with an accident blocking both lanes.

*I'm so glad Mom is driving, not me,* JoJo thought.

She closed her eyes, but then the aches seemed to worsen with each slight bump on the road, so she opened her eyes to focus on the trees as they passed them. *That's an elm, a maple, a blue spruce.* Her father taught her this game as they traveled between doctor visits and hospital stays. She learned to pick out leaf and bark textures and basic tree shapes from a distance.

*Trees are like my dad: solid, strong, tall,* JoJo thought, *I miss him so much.*

"We're almost there, Honey," Belinda said. With two more turns they pulled into the radiologist's office.

The women in the office did not allow Belinda to go back with JoJo.

"You'll be okay, JoJo," Belinda said as JoJo handed her the piece of paper with the band director's phone number. "I'll be here for you."

Back in a chilly room, the women positioned JoJo, covered her with heavy barriers for protection, asked her to hold very still and walked out.

*I feel so lonely,* JoJo thought, while closing her eyes. She found nothing interesting about the cold, barren room to focus on or to distract her mind.

When the women walked back in and removed the heavy coverings, JoJo thanked them and found her way back to her mother.

"Do we have any ice cream?" JoJo asked.

"Of course! Let's go," Belinda said.

On the way home, her mother said Mr. McCluggage expected her not to attend the game.

"He wants you to rest and to feel better soon," she said. "Also, Dr. Heim said an on-call radiologist will read the X-rays and will contact him. Then Dr. Heim will call them to to talk about what should happen next.

"We need to wait for the process to work, and it's unlikely for all of this to happen before the uniform call," Belinda said.

*This is such a helpless feeling,* JoJo thought. *There's nothing I can do about it. Maybe it's for the best. I feel so tired.*

Belinda swung the car into the driveway, parked and helped JoJo get out and stand up.

"I can get your things later," she said. "Let's get you situated first."

"Mom, am I allowed to eat?" JoJo asked as they walked up the steps onto the porch.

"Oh, no. You're right. Maybe you shouldn't eat if you might have a broken bone. I don't know," her mother said, opening the door. "We are supposed to alternate between ice and no ice until we hear. And I'm allowed to give you some acetaminophen for the pain and swelling. I just need to keep track of what time and how much, just in case.

"Can we stick with clear liquids until we hear from Dr. Heim?" Belinda asked.

"Sure," JoJo said. "I feel exhausted. Am I allowed to take a nap?"

"Yes, Darling. Let me throw a comforter on the couch and get your pillow. Then I'll keep track of the ice bags while you rest."

JoJo watched her mother set up a stenographer's notebook with columns for "time" and "action." And as JoJo eased onto the couch, she snuggled into the thick comforter as it it were giving her a huge soft hug. Belinda turned on a television documentary about a jungle, and JoJo fell asleep to screaming monkeys in treetops and cockatoos bobbing their heads.

# 23
# RESULTS

Trustworthy must be tested

When JoJo awakened the sun had set and the room was darkened except for the television, which played a different documentary about elephants in Africa and India.

"Thank you so much, Doctor," Belinda was saying. "That certainly is good news. We couldn't hope for much better. Thank you."

*I hurt all over,* JoJo thought, *should I move or just stay still? I can't figure it out. I give up.*

"Oh, you're awake," Belinda said, smiling kindly. "How are you feeling?"

"Sore," JoJo said. "What did Dr. Heim say?"

"Well, it looks like there are no broken bones, but you will be sore for some time," Belinda said. "The bone might be bruised, but they don't know yet. So you can eat now. And we can continue acetaminophen for the pain and swelling. Shall we indulge in dessert first?"

"Indeed!" JoJo said as they laughed together. "Let's celebrate!"

About a minute later, JoJo's mother returned from the kitchen with two of her grandmother's cut glass dessert dishes laden with ice cream, chocolate, whipped cream and brightly colored sprinkles.

"This was totally premeditated," Belinda said, smiling. "Hoping for the best, praying for the best, and we got it. Your favorite pizza is in the oven, too."

"Thank you, Mom," JoJo said. "You're the best!" She paused, "Mom?"

"What, JoJo."

"Tomorrow after you get off work, can we please go to our talking spot?"

"You mean at the beach?"

"Yes."

"Of course, Dear."

"Thank you. There's something important I need to tell you."

# 24

# EXPECTATIONS

See this acorn? It grows into an oak tree, but only if we plant it.

JoJo awoke to a dense fog smudging a familiar view of two scraggly cedar treetops outside her bedroom window. She felt overwhelming soreness every time she moved, so for a long time she didn't move.

Eventually she reached over to her bedside table with her good right arm and pulled Alice's Bible to her. She opened it and propped it up on a stuffed lion beside her.

"Help me hold it, Rory," she said.

As she slowly read aloud the first few Psalms, it wasn't long before she felt a connection with David, credited with authoring Psalm 3.

"Oh, Lord, how many are my foes!"

She read the passage through several times, then prayed, "God, I'm overwhelmed. I don't know what to do. And I hurt. Please, help!"

JoJo slowly sat up on the edge of the bed, then stood up. With her mother at work, she was not looking forward to attempting to get dressed by herself.

*Funny how I always took that for granted,* JoJo thought, as she held onto the banister with her right arm and lowered herself down one stair at a time. *This may be slow, but it's a lot better than the alternative.*

She shook her head against the thought of falling.

*I've never been this sore before, but moving seems to help a little.*

After the bottom step JoJo raised her good arm in a victory circle above her head.

"I made it! Oh, yeah!"

In the kitchen, JoJo found a note from her mother:

> "Dear JoJo.
>
> The cereal is in a bowl in the fridge, along with cut strawberries and milk in a glass and a cup of juice. The milk in the measuring cup is for your cereal. When you were a baby, your father used to do this for me every day, since I would be holding you when we got up.
>
> "For lunch, there are two pieces of pizza on a plate with a paper plate as a lid. Leave the paper plate on top until after you microwave the pizza for one minute, and let it sit for about five minutes. More milk with the pizza would be a good idea, to help your body recover.
>
> "There are two doses of acetaminophen, one for breakfast and one for four hours later.
>
> "I hope you feel better. Hoping for the best, but Dr. Heim said the soreness probably would get worse before it gets better. So don't freak out if it is worse today.
>
> "Call me if you need me.
>
> "Love, Mom."

*This is love,* JoJo thought. *Mom didn't have to do any of this. But you know what? It does make a difference. Little things matter.*

JoJo took the first dose of medicine and wrote down the time: 10 a.m.

*I can't believe I slept this late,* JoJo thought, stopping short of scolding herself. *I probably needed the extra rest.*

She pulled the cereal, milk, strawberries and juice out of the refrigerator, amazed at how an act of love could improve how she felt so much.

But then again, that was always her mom's and dad's life secret. No matter what horrible things happened to them, they chose to meet it with love. It covered everything -- treatments, setbacks celebrations -- everything.

*The medicine and breakfast helped,* JoJo thought as she rose to rinse the dishes and set them by the sink. *Now to figure out how to get dressed.*

But that, too, was thought through by her mother. After JoJo pulled her way up the stairs, on a chair in the bathroom was a pair of sweatpants, and one of her dad's sweatshirts. Her mom knew she loved that shirt. And it was big enough for her to pull over her head and ease the sore arm into it.

In the shower, JoJo saw there were more bruises than she thought the night before.

*Everything happened so fast,* JoJo thought. *I wonder if anyone else got hurt.*

Even though she set the spray of water in the shower to its softest setting, it hurt. So she turned the water off, lathered up, and turned it on again to rinse off as quickly as possible.

She dressed, picked out her hair, found soft footies in her drawer, pulled one on each foot with one hand and headed back downstairs.

*One more thing,* JoJo thought. She found her dad's CD of classical music, opened the drawer of the player and inserted the disc, pushed the drawer in and pressed, "Play."

"That's better," she said. "Now to tackle homework."

JoJo moved her books a couple at a time to the kitchen table, then remembered she needed to put ice on the bruised elbow and arm. So she held a plastic bag up to the ice maker on the fridge, filled it, sealed it, wrapped it in a hand towel and stuck it in the sleeve of the sweatshirt. Then she set that arm on the table and started the algebra again.

*I can focus better this time,* she thought, as she solved the first equation, then the second. Then she thought she heard a knock at the door.

*That's funny,* JoJo thought. *I'm not expecting anyone.*

When she walked into the dining room and looked out of the window, she couldn't see anyone standing on the porch, nor vehicles parked on the street. She walked up to the door, clutching the ice bag, and looked out. There on the porch were balloons, teddy bears and a basket full of notes.

"What?" JoJo exclaimed, astonished. Then Alice walked up the sidewalk carrying a covered casserole dish. JoJo opened the door for her.

"It looks like you had some visits from friends," Alice said.

JoJo, smiling with tears in her eyes, welcomed Alice inside, showing her to the kitchen to set down the casserole.

"This is my favorite," Alice said.

She handed JoJo a recipe card.

Green Bean and Tater Casserole

Brown 1 pound of hamburger, crumble, spread in bottom of dish
Drain a can of green beans, spread on hamburger
Spread a can of cream of mushroom soup on the beans
Add a layer of frozen taters on top
Bake at 350 degrees for one hour.

"Oh! That does sound good," JoJo said, while opening the door of the refrigerator so Alice could set it inside.

"Now let me bring in those other things," Alice said.

"Wait," said JoJo. "Can we take a picture of it first?"

"Of course," Alice said.

"Did you see who brought them?" JoJo asked while Alice picked up the items and carried them inside.

"No, I didn't," Alice said. "It looks like the balloons and the basket of cards are from the band. And notes with the bears each say, 'Hope you're feeling better, from a Secret Admirer,' in different handwriting."

"That could be good or bad," JoJo said. They laughed.

"Well, you have plenty of time to figure that out," Alice said. "It doesn't have to be this weekend. How are you feeling?"

"Just plain sore," JoJo said, "but also amazed that anyone would go to the trouble to reach out like this. Would you like to have a seat? I could make you a cup of tea."

"A cup of tea sounds lovely, but I came to help you," Alice said.

"I can still do some things," JoJo said.

She placed the ice bag in the freezer and filled a tea kettle at the faucet. While the water heated on the stove, JoJo opened a couple of the notes. And they were written by band members.

"I hope you're feeling better. Brad. Trumpet"

"We're so sorry about what happened to you today. Krystal. Drums."

The tea kettle whistle started low then increased in pitch as JoJo turned off the stove and the burner slowly cooled.

JoJo reached up for the China tea cups that belonged to her grandmother, along with saucers and teaspoons. She offered a small basket with an assortment of teas in individual bags to Alice, and brought the cups to the table.

"I'm pouring at the table," JoJo said. "I'm not sure about carrying the cups full of hot water. Oh! Do you like cardamom cookies? Mom just baked some."

"Yes, I do," Alice said. "My grandmother used to bake them regularly. It's one of my fondest memories of her."

JoJo brought the cookie tin, and Alice opened it. They each chose two cookies and closed the tin again. They bowed their heads together.

"Dear Heavenly Father, Thank you for tea and cookies and friends, in Jesus' name, amen," Alice prayed.

"So, what exactly happened yesterday?" Alice asked, "And I mean, the whole day. I was asked to pray for you early in the morning, and I did. But what happened?"

JoJo sighed. As much as she loved Alice, she hadn't really talked about this with her mother yet. Still, her mother heard about some of it in the doctor's office. And those bruises were really blue today. So as they munched and sipped together, JoJo spoke and Alice listened.

"Someone stacked my locker, and that never happened to me before and I wasn't ready for it, and it really hurt," JoJo said. "But I think the mean laughter hurt more. Then the book report I wrote after choir practice was gone. Mrs. Smith was nice...I can turn it in Monday. Even so, I felt like I was sinking into so much hurtfulness and I didn't know how to pull myself out of it. Just having your locker stacked isn't that big of a deal, and I can't explain why I felt the way I did, and it felt so helpless."

Alice quietly listened as JoJo explained about meeting Sharon while catching grasshoppers and not being able to complete even one algebra problem. Then the "Big Trip" in front of everybody.

"I don't know how or who did it," JoJo said, "but everyone after that has been amazingly kind to me. Kindness makes all the difference."

"Well spoken," Alice said. "Would it be all right if I pray with you?"

JoJo nodded, and they held hands with Alice's right hand on top of JoJo's sore left hand ever so gently.

"Loving Heavenly Father, Thank you so much for JoJo. We don't understand how you do it, but you can make good come out of bad things that happen to our loved ones. Thank you for the beauty you placed within JoJo. Thank you for caring tenderly for her, and watching over her. And thank you for Belinda. Please let your healing presence rest on them both, and fill them with your great joy, because your joy is our strength. In Jesus' precious name we pray, Amen."

***

While JoJo put away the tea and cookies and carried the cups and saucers to the sink, Alice sent a text, "JoJo served tea and cookies. It just might work, after all."

# 25

# REMEMBER LONG

Wait for rising drafts.

After JoJo and Alice hugged and said, "Good-bye," JoJo returned to the basket of notes. Some were funny; others, kind.

The sentiments lifted some of the loneliness that added to her suffering.

She returned to the homework and solved most of the problems easily.

Then she decided on a late lunch because of the late breakfast and snack with Alice. After heating and eating the pizza, she took the medicine and sat down to rewrite the book report for Mrs. Smith.

But rather than focusing on the story about Ginny and Jerry, her mind wandered to a conversation with her father she had forgotten, partly because of the pain of his death a couple of months later.

"JoJo, I've been praying for you," her father said. "And I want to make sure you have the right focus, even through tough times."

"What do you mean, Dad?"

"Well, for now you have me and your mom," he explained. "We watch out for you and we love you to pieces. But you need other people, good people, in your life, too. And sometimes it's hard to figure out who the good people are. Sometimes people look good on the outside, but they're mean as snakes on the inside. Sometimes people don't seem quite right on the outside, but you never know. They might be a good person who is going through something very, very hard. And maybe they never thought it would happen to them, so they're upset. They might still be good people...good people struggling.

"I guess what I'm trying to say is, even if something were to happen to me or to your mom, find good people, a good place to belong," her dad said with such a serious expression on his face it almost frightened her. "They can help you be strong, JoJo. Belong, be strong."

He hugged her close and just held her for awhile. She relaxed under his strong arms and welcome embrace. She could hear his heart beating steady and strong.

*I felt so loved in that moment,* JoJo recalled, with tears welling into her eyes.

"Daddy, I belong to you and Mom," she had said to him. He smiled, but something in his eyes seemed sad.

*He must have known then,* JoJo thought. *He and Mom knew that long ago that the fight was lost. Or if they didn't know, they suspected it.*

Alone in the house, JoJo didn't need to choke back the tears that finally fell in a torrent of grief and despair. She left her books as they were, rose and hoisted herself up the stairs, grabbing a box of tissues from the bathroom.

*I need these,* she decided.

JoJo sobbed until she was done, no more tears left. She drifted into an exhausted sleep.

# 26

# DREAM

Look for signs, clues, lines, glues.

As JoJo lay dreaming, she heard faint clicks of a key distantly turning in a metal lock and the big wooden front door open with a squawk.

"JoJo?" her mother called gently. Not quiet awake, JoJo heard her mother's footsteps as she walked through the dining room to the kitchen and back to the bottom of the stairs.

Slowly awakening, JoJo tried to stretch her arms above her head, but the pain of the bruises cut short the attempt.

"I'm here," JoJo called, as her mother climbed the stairs.

"How are you doing, Honey?" Belinda asked as she looked into the doorway and walked into JoJo's room.

"Sore. It's a lot worse today. And the bruises are really ugly," JoJo said. "Mom, when you came home I was having the funniest dream. There was this little armadillo, and she was running in little circles, and she had this long blonde hair, like a long-haired dachshund. And every now and then she would run over to me and lean against my leg so I could pet her head and her blonde hair. Then she would tear off, running in circles again."

85

Belinda smiled and shook her head.

"That one is really different," she said, laughing. "Do armadillos have hair?"

"I don't know, but this one did," JoJo said, also laughing.

"An armadillo," Belinda said pensively. "They have protection in their tough exterior. You need protection."

"Is that what the dream meant?" JoJo asked.

"I don't know. It just hit me," Belinda said. "And I'm not really sure how I can protect you, or I would. I've been feeling like I want to yank you out of that school. But I'm not sure if that's the correct response.

"JoJo, last night you asked if we could go to the talking spot today," Belinda said. "Do you still want to go there? Do you feel up to it?"

"I am really sore, Mom, but when I get moving it seems to help a little bit," JoJo said. "But I want you to know, I am really, really slow. And I"m not much help. But I have one good arm."

Belinda smiled at her.

"Darling, you take your time," she said. "Everything will work out fine."

"Mom, Alice stopped by," JoJo said. "She brought a casserole for supper. And we had tea. And guess what? There were teddy bears and a basket and balloons on the front porch."

"I know," her mother said. "They were there this morning when I went to work. I left them there because I thought it would be more fun for you to find them."

"All this time I was trying to be friends with people who didn't want me around," JoJo said, "and they were cruel. When all along I could have been friends with other people. Why couldn't I see it?"

"Right time, right place. Maybe you needed to be ready to see it," Belinda said. "JoJo, by asking to go to the talking spot, you're letting me know what we need to talk about is serious, right?"

"Yes, Mom. It's very serious," JoJo said. "I don't know that it will take a long time. I don't know what to say or do. I just need to tell you."

"Okay," Belinda said. "I appreciate that you're asking to talk. I want to know what you have to say. How about if we get milkshakes as snacks along the way. The ice cream shop is still open, right? Then we can have supper later.

"Wash up. It looks like you had a good cry," Belinda said, gently again.

"You could tell?" JoJo asked, incredulous.

"I'm the mom," Belinda replied with a mock serious expression and both fists on her hips.

"Right," JoJo said, smiling.

# 27

# THE TALKING SPOT

Let truth, respect and love season every conversation.

When Belinda swung the car into a parking spot at a beach almost a half-hour away from their home, she parked and they both grabbed their hand-crafted milkshakes as they exited the car.

It rarely happened that they chose the same flavor of milkshake. Usually they bought different shakes, and shared so they could enjoy more than one "taste escape," they called it. But this day mom and daughter requested Triple Chocolate Everything in their huge cups.

It had been a tough few days.

JoJo nestled her milkshake in the crook of her arm and held out her hand for her beach chair, while Belinda tossed their special blanket on her arm, rested her chair on her side, picked up her milkshake and closed the trunk lid. She picked up her chair and they headed across the parking lot to the opposite end of the beach from where people usually congregated, so they could listen to the waves lapping at an outcropping of rocks and along the sandy shore.

Two gulls faced off in a squawky squabble, flapping their wings and practically screaming at each other.

JoJo and Belinda watched, bemused, until the birds flew off a few minutes later and circled high overhead.

Belinda settled her chair into the thick sand of the beach, then turned to where JoJo struggled to open her chair. Together they set it into the sand next to Belinda's chair, sat down and shared the special blanket, a gift from Alice and in a way, JoJo's dad.

*How do I start?* JoJo thought. *What should I say first?*

JoJo ran her fingers over the soft flannel fabrics on the top side, knowing well the different colored denim patches on the underneath.

Alice had visited months after JoJo's dad died, and had seen a stack of his shirts and pants on a dining room chair. Belinda meant to take them to a homeless shelter or something, she said, but just couldn't, yet. It was still too hard.

So Alice asked for them, and asked if she could use them in any way she liked. Belinda granted permission.

JoJo had been upset as she heard what she considered an offensive request.

*And why didn't Mom ask if I was ready to give up the clothes? I wasn't,* JoJo recalled. Her heart hurt from it, but she didn't say anything.

Then months later, Alice returned with the special quilt. Her dad's soft, colorful flannel shirts were cut into four-inch squares and arranged in nine-patch patterns. On the back his jeans had been cut into larger squares and rectangles, and stitched together. Then both sides were sewn together. Alice spent hours and weeks working on the special quilt for them. And they both knew she prayed for them while she cut and sewed.

The mom and daughter sat quietly for some time, a custom at the talking spot.

Then JoJo, the one who asked for the home meeting, started the conversation with a short prayer.

"Loving Heavenly Father," JoJo prayed. "Please be with us and help us as we talk things out. And please give Dad a hug for both of us. We love you. In Jesus' name, amen."

JoJo looked up. Belinda waited quietly.

"Mom, I've told you most of what happened this week," JoJo said. "But even before I tripped, I was struggling with something else. I couldn't concentrate. I couldn't think. I felt numb. It seemed like when they stacked my locker and those books hit me so hard and knocked my breath out, something else was knocked out of me. Or maybe the pain from the mean girls' rejection hit rock bottom. I couldn't dig my way out of it with happy thoughts or little sayings.

"And it scared me. I didn't know what to do."

Belinda listened quietly, which was the rule. And she waited.

"I'm done," JoJo said, starting to tear up again at the memory and the overwhelming rush of feelings.

"You were right," Belinda said. "we did need to come to the talking spot for this."

Her mom leaned back in the chair and closed her eyes.

JoJo waited for her response, which was also a talking spot rule. All people need to give God a chance to guide them and to guide their words, they decided as a family, especially in the talking spot.

The gulls circled lower. One dove for a small fish near the surface of the huge lake.

JoJo sipped her milkshake. *It's hard to drink with a lump in your throat,* she thought.

Though it was later in the afternoon and a bit chilly with a brisk breeze off the lake, she became increasingly aware of people walking from the parking lot and carrying things to the opposite end of the beach.

"JoJo," her mother said. "Is it okay for us to go to counseling, either together or separately? This might be too big for me."

JoJo nodded, thinking, *I know it's too big for me.*

"I mean, you were right to tell me, and I'm so thankful you did," Belinda said. "But I don't know how to help. And right now, I'm not sure who to ask. But I'll ask around and do my best to find someone quickly. And I do care. I'm so thankful you told me. Your asking for us to come here was the best thing you could have done.

"But how do you feel about going back to school?" Belinda asked.

JoJo waited before she spoke.

"Part of me is scared, so scared I feel like choking when I think about it," JoJo said. "But part of me wants to face this with dignity, like Dad taught me. He faced his scary things with dignity.

"And then, there are all of the notes in the basket," JoJo said, looking directly at her mother. "None of them seemed forced, like when we were little and the teacher wrote a thank you note on the blackboard and we all copied it to send to hosts of a field trip or whatever. Maybe someone would like to be a friend, and would be a good friend. 'Belong, be strong,' Dad said. I belong to the band, to choir, to youth group.

"Mom, I want to be strong," JoJo said. "I'm just afraid of if they attack again, because I sank so low emotionally after my locker was stacked. And you know what? Having your locker stacked is not that big of a deal. It was just a prank.

But I couldn't pull myself up emotionally. That's why I felt I needed to tell you."

"JoJo, this makes all the sense in the world," Belinda said, kindly. "You have been through so much. I wish I could hug you, but I"m afraid I'll hurt you more."

"We could hold hands and pray," JoJo said. So they did. When they said, "Amen," and opened their eyes, probably 20 brightly colored kites bobbed happily in the sky.

"Mom, look!" JoJo exclaimed. They both giggled.

More kites were on the way up, each coaxed into the breeze by a team of two, one person holding the kite, and the other person standing upwind, holding the string taut. At a signal, the one holding the kite let go and the other one wound up the string until the kite started lifting vertically, then let out the string at the right moment to let the kite soar, it's tail twisting and flapping in the breeze.

A woman walked toward Belinda and JoJo, holding a bright purple kite with a long colorful tail in her right hand, and a ball of string in her left hand.

"Is that Alice?" JoJo asked.

Belinda smiled and said, "I believe so."

# 28

# CLUB KINDNESS

Look for the good 'cause God is all around us, and what he created is good

Alice walked up to Belinda and JoJo with a huge grin on her face.

"Hello!" they all exclaimed.

"JoJo, how are you feeling?" Alice asked.

"Sore, but better in a way," JoJo said.

"Yes," Belinda said. "It was very good for us to come to the talking spot."

"JoJo, the Kite Club saw what happened yesterday," Alice said, "and they would like to extend to you the Friend Kite. You may not feel like flying it today, but they want you to have it."

"A Friend Kite?" JoJo asked.

"The club started years ago," Alice explained. "Two brothers were flying kites, and a boy walked up to them, asking questions. Finally he said, 'I wish I had a kite,' and walked away. Both boys wished they had thought quickly enough to give him a kite. They never saw him again, but they decided never again to fly kites without a Friend Kite to give to someone.

"So," Alice said, "will you accept a Friend Kite from the Kite Club? It doesn't mean you have to join. It just means, join or not, you're a friend. And if you're at a place where they are flying, you're welcome to fly kites with them."

JoJo looked at Belinda, who smiled and nodded.

"Yes," JoJo said. "I will accept the Friend Kite. Will someone fly it for me? Will someone teach me how to fly it? I thought you had to run to fly a kite, but they aren't running."

"Some of the students said they are acquainted with you," Alice said, "and you met the gym teacher yesterday. He is one of the brothers. His brother is a gym teacher at another school district, and sometimes their kite clubs get together for regional kite flying events. My husband belonged to a kite club for adults. Some of them travel all over the country with stunt kites.

"The club here today gets together during bad weather or on calm days to build kites, so they always have a few Friend Kites to give away," Alice said. "A girl named Sharon received a Friend Kite last week, and she is here today. She's one of the ones who said she's acquainted with you."

"Yes, I met Sharon yesterday, catching grasshoppers," JoJo said. "It seems like that was so long ago."

"Do you feel up to meeting the club?" Alice asked.

"Yes, as long as no one touches me," JoJo said. "I don't think they would intentionally hurt me, but I'm so sore all over."

"Fair enough," Alice said.

As they walked toward the group, JoJo and Belinda tossed their empty cups in a trash can and JoJo wrapped up in the special blanket while Belinda carried the chairs.

"Thank you so much for the Friend Kite! It's so pretty!" JoJo exclaimed.

Sharon introduced JoJo to the students she knew, and the others chimed in with their names.

The gym teacher, George, explained some basics about flying kites: "Wait for the breeze, then release the kite and wind the string up to make it climb, then as it tugs release string to allow it to soar."

He and Sharon demonstrated with JoJo's Friend Kite until it climbed about 30 feet, then George handed the string to JoJo. She felt the tension on the string, with the wind tugging and tugging.

"I feel like I could fly away with it," JoJo said quietly as she gazed at the kite.

She turned and handed the string to George.

"Thank you so much! Now how do you get it to come down?" JoJo asked.

"One thing to remember is: Kites come down; it's what they do. Just don't take it personally," George said. He let out some string to release tension and walked with the wind. The purple kite fluttered and dove down into the sand. He rolled up the string as he walked to it, then picked up the kite and handed it to JoJo.

"Hope you're feeling better soon," he said, smiling.

"Thank you," JoJo said. "Thank you for being so kind. This was such a surprise. And your kites are so beautiful. Mrs. Stacey said you make them? They're so pretty."

George grinned, bowed his head and waved, "You're welcome. Get better soon."

"Thank you. This was so kind of all of you all," Belinda said, smiling. "God bless you."

JoJo felt happy, yet tired as they walked to the car. She hadn't expected so much to happen. Exhausted, she just wanted to rest.

"Let's go home and fix that casserole," Belinda said. "I asked Alice to join us, but she said she had another commitment."

"Sounds good, Mom," JoJo said, trying not to fall asleep in the car with the warm sunshine splashing in the window and all over her.

When they were almost home, her mother said, "JoJo, I've been thinking. You may be making friends at school now. Those seemed like nice young people. But that does not mean you're safe at school if the bullying continues.

"I'm going with you on Monday. We can walk in together, then I need to talk to the principal," she said. "Maybe someone else saw what happened at the assembly, or who stacked your locker."

She pulled the car into the driveway.

"I need to get to the bottom of this."

# 29

# FAMILY TRAIT

Do the math: Thankful = Happy

If JoJo were not so sore, and a little bit afraid to go to school, then she might have objected to her mother's plan. But then again, JoJo had been trying to figure this out practically since school started for the year, and the weather already was turning cool. She realized she cannot handle this on her own.

Some things need extra help.

Exhausted, JoJo settled down in a kitchen chair in front of the school books just to "Doe ye nexte thynge," as her mother's small plaque over the kitchen sink quipped in Old English.

*Ye nexte thynge,* JoJo thought, is algebra problem number 17.

Belinda checked the oven for pans, then turned the knobs to preheat at 350 degrees. She retrieved Alice's casserole from the fridge and set it on the counter, reading the note on the top of it.

"Sounds delicious," Belinda said, as JoJo began copying the second problem for the evening. Several problems later, the oven preheat light clicked off and Belinda placed the casserole on a center rack.

"Supper will be in about an hour," Belinda said. "How are you feeling?"

"Tired, but good," JoJo said, thankful to have worked through so many math problems.

*I might even finish them today,* she thought.

"Do you need any help?" Belinda asked.

"Not right now. Yesterday I did. But more than you know, you have helped so much already," JoJo said. "Mom, I should have told you when you got home. Your notes this morning and the extra things you did for me really made a difference when I got up. It helped so much! Thank you. I really felt loved. I mean, I know you love me every day, but in those frustrating early moments, I felt truly loved. Thank you."

Belinda listened and smiled.

"JoJo, your father taught me that," she said quietly.

"So now it's a family trait," JoJo said. They looked at each other, and laughed.

"Mom, I want to be just like you."

# 30

## REST

If you catch a toad look at him and let him go. He eats bugs.

After supper JoJo wasn't much help with the dishes, but she tried. She covered the casserole and set it in the fridge, then put away the ketchup and mustard, margarine and jelly.

Belinda had raced around the house for the hour before they ate, sorting laundry, filling the washing machine, then the dryer, running the vacuum and dusting.

The dishes, also, were accomplished quickly. Then Belinda opened the roll top desk and began opening bills she arranged by due date in a stack.

"Mom?" JoJo said. "Is it okay if I go to bed now?"

"Of course it is," Belinda said, looking up into her daughter's eyes. "How are you doing?"

"I'm okay, just exhausted," JoJo said. "I took a nap today, so I can't believe I'm this tired.

"Well, your body needs to rebuild itself," Belinda said. "JoJo, is it okay if I see the bruises?"

"Um, yes. But they're ugly," JoJo said.

Upstairs in the bathroom, JoJo pulled the sweatshirt sleeve from her sore arm, and Belinda looked at the swelling, and the purple bruises. JoJo was not able to stretch out her arm yet, and she had not been using her left hand at all.

Her mother frowned, pensively.

"Dr. Heim said it would be a while before the swelling would go down," Belinda said. "And it probably will be sore for a very long time, maybe weeks."

"Mom, can I still play in the band?" JoJo asked.

"Let's wait and see," she replied.

The other bruises had been a raging red, but now they were hard and purple.

"It's amazing there were no broken bones," Belinda said. "I'm thankful for that. But we also need to listen to your body. And you probably do need extra rest...and extra nutrition, come to think of it. Do you need help getting ready for bed?"

"Is it okay if I just wear Dad's sweatshirt for tonight? I'll change the sweatpants," JoJo said.

"Sure," Belinda said. "While you're doing that, I'm going to run to the store for some protein shakes. The extra nutrition could only help. What flavor would you like?"

"Chocolate for sure."

"Coming right up," Belinda said, as she walked quickly down the stairs, grabbed her purse and headed out the door.

Light lingered outside as early whisps of a sunset smudged the western horizon. JoJo could not remember the last time she had gone to bed so early. But her body insisted rest was her "nexte thynge."

# 31

# SUNDAY

*Eagles fly a certain way.*

"JoJo, Darling."

In the middle of another crazy dream, JoJo heard her mother's gentle voice, rousing her.

But at first she thought her mother was in the dream, breaking into her subconscious to help foil a diabolical plot twisting constantly against her.

"JoJo, Darling."

She stirred, opened her eyes.

"Mom?" She rolled onto her right side.

"What time is it? Is it still Saturday?"

"No, it's Sunday morning, Darling. Are you going to church today? It's 8 a.m. and choir meets at 9:30."

The choir always warmed up and then prayed together before Sunday school started, then ran through the choir number once after the classes and before the service.

"Wow." was the only thing JoJo could say at first. Then she added, "Yes."

After another few moments, a second realization emerged, "Mom, what should I wear?"

Well, I was thinking something comfortable and soft," Belinda said. "Last evening it turned cold in a hurry. We even had frost on the ground this morning."

"Soft warm sweater... How about my blue one, and plaid pants? They're soft, not too tight, and no zipper or buttons," JoJo said.

As JoJo sat up on the bed, Belinda retrieved the clothes from her drawers and closet, and placed them in the bathroom.

"Do you want me to wash your hair? We can do it in the kitchen sink before your shower."

"That's a good idea," JoJo said.

After JoJo attended to toiletries, she lowered herself down the stairs. She leaned on her good elbow while lowering her head to the sink. Her mother massaged her scalp and hair with the suds and rinsed quickly, added conditioner and rinsed again.

*I couldn't have washed my hair that fast,* JoJo thought, *not even in the shower.*

For breakfast Belinda blended a protein shake with some chocolate ice cream, and handed JoJo more acetaminophen to ease the pain and swelling.

"I'd better hurry," JoJo said. She pulled herself back up the stairs and into the bathroom for a shower.

After she pulled on her clothes and picked out her hair, she grabbed her socks and shoes and lowered herself back down the stairs. Belinda smiled at her.

"You look beautiful in that color," she said. "It's a good color for you."

"Thanks, Mom."

"Would you like some omelet and some juice? We still have about 15 minutes before we need to leave. And your hair could dry a little bit."

"That sounds great. I would like some omelet, thanks."
"I made your favorite," Belinda said, beaming.

# 32

# POSITIVE

Get a breath of fresh air.

The drive to the little country church included squinting through morning sun on their faces, even while wearing sunglasses.

Along the way, JoJo realized her friends from church, other than Alice, did not know about the incidents at school. They all attended her old school.

"Mom, what should I tell my friends at church?"

"How much do you want to tell them?"

"I'm sore, and I don't want anyone to hug me or jostle me or whatever," she said.

"How about saying it in a positive way, like in a request for them to pray for you for healing because you're so sore all over?" Belinda recommended. "We can start with the choir, then after they pray for you, you can ask your friends in Sunday school for prayer.

"JoJo, someone might forget, like one of the kids," Belinda said. "Decide ahead of time to forgive them, to not hold it against them."

"Is that what Dad did?"

"Yes, and it made all the difference. There were times he needed to extend that forgiveness to me and you, and I didn't even know it until much later, when he was able to talk about it."

"Oh, I never knew," JoJo said, turning to her mother. "I'm going to choose that road, too, since it was good enough for Dad."

# 33

## LOVED

*Choose joy, it's more fun.*

From a distance JoJo could see the tall, square bell tower rising above the trees and buildings around it where the church sat on the top of a small hill.

An old elementary school building, turned into apartments, nestled next to the church, and beside the school, a very old cemetery.

Even though that was where her father was buried that harshly cold, rainy day of his funeral, he wasn't there. She knew her father was in heaven. And he didn't hurt any more. That was the best part. She loved her father, but she couldn't bear for him to suffer any longer, no matter how much it hurt to lose him.

Since it took time for JoJo to climb the stairs of the red brick building built in the 1800s, her mother went into the choir room first. As JoJo arrived, Belinda was briefly explaining about the accident at school, and asking for prayer over JoJo.

"A couple of people can place a hand on her back," Belinda said, "but please avoid her left arm and elbow. That's still very sore."

The choir members gathered around JoJo, who by then was seated on a chair. After the prayers began, JoJo felt warm all over, like when she took a relaxing bath. Their familiar voices called lovingly on God to heal their JoJo, to bring his grace and wisdom into her life with a healing flood of forgiveness into her soul.

*Loved,* JoJo thought. *I feel loved. I belong.*

They spoke blessings over her, and by the time the first, "Amen," was whispered, she knew their prayers were heard and answered by their eternally good God.

"Thank you so much!" JoJo said, wishing she could hug them each.

Rosemary offered to share music with JoJo while they ran through the number and sang a hushed benediction. Then she walked to the youth class.

There, she stood in the doorway as two boys jostled over an eraser and Leana drew pink hearts on a chalkboard.

"How do you know when it's true love?" was written at the top of the board by their teacher, Mr. Gene Schoolcraft.

"Come in, JoJo," he called. "The boys paused their rough-housing.

"Well, I need to ask a favor," JoJo said. "Will you please pray for me?"

She told briefly about the accident, the bruises, and the soreness.

"Oh, I'm sorry that happened to you. Yes, we will," Mr. Schoolcraft said. "We would be honored to pray for you."

She sat down. Mr. Schoolcraft had Leana touch JoJo on the back. The rest held hands while Mr. Schoolcraft prayed.

"Loving Heavenly Father," he prayed. "You're so huge, and we're so small, yet you reach down to touch us, to help us in our need. Please wrap JoJo in your loving arms, help her feel your tender love and care, and help her know you are always near. Please show her your love and healing presence. Thank you, God, in Jesus' name we pray. Amen."

"Mr. Schoolcraft," Leana said, "if God is always near, then why didn't he keep JoJo from getting hurt?"

"Oh, but we think he did," JoJo blurted out. "Mom said she was amazed I wasn't hurt worse. It was a hard fall with all of my weight on my left elbow. And I got stepped on. I don't have broken bones. It could have been so much worse.

"And since then, people have been so kind to me."

"Those are good points, JoJo," Mr. Schoolcraft said. "But let's go a little deeper. Even if the worst had happened, God is still near. There are things we cannot understand apart from a view toward eternity. We don't understand suffering. We don't understand death. But God can use both of those awful things for good of those who love Him.

"And there are some things pain teaches us, that we can't learn any other way," Mr. Schoolcraft said.

"I was always lonely at my new school," JoJo said, "but after the accident people have been so kind to me."

She explained about her mother's notes and breakfast, the surprises on the porch, Mrs. Stacey's visit and the Friend Kite.

"You know, the Kite Club did not just respond to the accident," JoJo said. "They thought ahead, and made extra kites to give away as Friend Kites to whomever happened to be around. A girl I met Friday got a Friend Kite last week. And you don't have to join if you don't want to or if you can't. They give a Friend Kite, anyway."

"What do you think, class?" Mr. Schoolcraft asked. "Is this love?"

"It seems like an example of it," said Brent, who ended up with the eraser.

"Can you give other examples of true love? Remember, we're not talking about 'puppy love' or crushes. We're talking about lasting love that stands the test of time," Mr. Schoolcraft said.

"You know, I wrecked my bike once, really bad, and I was biking in a place Dad told me not to," Brent said, "but I didn't listen. I biffed and rolled down into a ravine. I couldn't move. My friend saw what happened and rode as fast as he could to get my dad. He came right away. He never said a word about my not being allowed to be there. We both knew. He just cared for me. He got me out of there, and took me to the hospital. I still have scars. But I felt loved. Even though I did something wrong and paid dearly for it, I felt loved."

"That's deep," Mr. Schoolcraft said. "Class, what if we continue the discussion next week? Bring any examples you see of real love. And, how can you tell it's real?"

They prayed, and the teens went to the sanctuary to sit with their families.

# 34
# WORTHY

*Be still and know God*

Only Thursday, during choir practice, JoJo sang the words of the anthem, but it was only a nice song with a sweet melody and challenging harmonies.

But now the words patterned from Psalm 5 sprang from her lips as a prayer, even in practice before the service.

"You are not a God who takes pleasure in evil," she sang, and realized that was what her mother and Alice were trying to say before Friday ever happened. "But I, by your great mercy, will come into your house, in reverence I bow down before you. Lord lead me, lead me in your righteousness. Because my enemies distress, let me seek you first, worthy to honor and bless."

*A heart song is different from just a song,* JoJo thought. *And God is worthy of heart songs.*

When they finished rehearsing, Belinda held JoJo's choir robe so she could ease her arms into it, then fastened a hook at the top and zipped it up. She looked into JoJo's eyes.

"Are you still okay?"

"Yes."

They both followed the rest of the choir up the steep steps and into the choir loft around the huge old organ.

Mrs. Stacey slid across the large wooden bench, flipped on the small metal switch, pulled out the stops to set the tone of the organ for the introduction and paused, like she did each time, for a prayer to her loving God, an offering of worship to Him.

Then the music began.

# 35

# BULLSEYE

Look for ways to show kindness, then do it.

During the first part of the worship service, JoJo was feeling closer and closer to God. Then Pastor Don's choice of scripture and sermon topic stunned her.

"Turn to Luke 6:27," Pastor Don said. "'But I tell you who hear me: Love your enemies; do good to those who hate you. Bless those who curse you, pray for those who mistreat you...'"

*Did someone tell him about school?* JoJo wondered. She felt her face becoming hot, and she appreciated her seat behind a banner between the choir and congregation, so no one could see her discomfort.

"*Love your enemies*," JoJo thought. *But what if my enemies don't want me to love them? That's the problem.*

Pastor Don went on to explain Christ's list of responses from us to our enemies:

- Love
- Do good
- Bless
- Pray for

"It's a simple list," Pastor Don said, "but it's not necessarily easy to carry out in real life. Let's ask God to help us."

He prayed for the congregation, for God's guidance in living the Word in a depraved, wicked world.

With the final, "Amen," Alice played the starting chord of the choir's benediction. After the solemn song, the congregation began filling out of the church, shaking Pastor Don's hand at the door and thanking him for his encouragement.

JoJo followed the rest of the choir into the choir room, but she felt shaken. Her mother bent in front of her to unhook the top of the robe and to unzip it.

"Mom," JoJo whispered. "Did you tell him about school?"

"Who, JoJo?" Belinda asked. "I told the choir and we prayed for you."

"Pastor Don," she said.

"No, I didn't call him yet," Belinda said. "He is one of the people I intend to call, but I haven't yet. Why do you ask?"

"Did he know about the list?" JoJo asked.

"No, not that I know of."

"It was like that sermon was just for me."

Belinda paused, and smiled without being unkind.

"JoJo, any time you feel a sermon is directed to you, assume it was God who directed it," Belinda said. "My mother told me that a long time ago. Now that you say that, it does fit your situation, doesn't it? I guess I was too busy applying it to my own life. I wasn't thinking about how it affected you.

"So what do you think? Is following the points Pastor Don laid out in the sermon doable in your case?" Belinda asked.

"I'm not sure," JoJo said. "How do you love people who don't want to be loved by you?"

"Well, for one thing, God knows how that feels, so you can ask Him," Belinda said. "Then until He shows you, do the other things on the list you are able to accomplish. Those are things we all need to practice."

"Mom, may I go talk to Pastor Don?" JoJo asked.

"Sure, Honey," Belinda said.

JoJo headed for the back of the sanctuary where Pastor Don was shaking hands with the last few parishioners as they left the church.

*I don't want to seem disrespectful,* JoJo thought, *still, I'm not sure how to approach the subject with Pastor Don.*

When she shook his hand she ended up blurting out, "Pastor Don, did you know about what was going on at my school this week?"

Pastor Don seemed startled. He smiled as he shook off the surprise, then looked tenderly at JoJo.

"Why, no, JoJo. I hadn't heard anything about your school this week," he said. "Why don't you come into my office and we can talk?"

He opened the door of his office and hung his long, heavy robe on a hanger and then on a special hook on the wall for it. He motioned for JoJo to sit in a soft fabric chair, then he sat across his desk in his wooden office chair that creaked when he sat down. He leaned forward and rested his elbows on his desk, with his hands clasped together in front of him.

"What happened, JoJo?" he asked gently.

As she told of her frustration with the girls and her loneliness, then the dirty tricks, and the incidents on Friday, he looked at her kindly and seemed to listen intently. He nodded at times.

When JoJo seemed done talking, Pastor Don sat back in his chair and said, "So, are you wondering if my sermon today was written just for you?"

JoJo nodded.

He smiled, paused and sighed.

"JoJo, I would never intentionally embarrass you from the pulpit," Pastor Don said. "I love you and all of the people here. If it thought you needed counsel or correction, I would take you aside and speak with you privately. As for the sermon, it was planned months ago in a special series on walking close with God and living the Christian life.

"That said, I was told when I was about your age, that if a pastor is preaching to you, listen and respond," he said. "It's not really from the pastor."

"It's from God?" she asked.

"Most probably," he said. "Though we are to test everything with scripture: What else is written in the Bible about that topic?"

"Then what do you do if your enemies don't want you to love them?" JoJo asked. "That's the problem."

"Follow God's list of responses to our enemies," he said. "God will do the rest. Trust Jesus."

While Pastor Don prayed for JoJo, she felt comforted and helped, and a peace settled in.

*God is working in my situation even if I can't see it yet,* she thought, *I read that in Alice's Bible.*

After the prayer Pastor Don looked up into her eyes.

"JoJo, I went through some difficult times when I was in school," he said. "So I can appreciate how tough your situation must be. I'm going to continue praying for you. Please feel free to let me know if you need specific prayer or counsel. You're not alone. I care about what you're going through."

"Thank you so much," JoJo said, as she got up and walked out of the office. Belinda and Alice stood outside the door, waiting for her.

"There you are," Belinda said. "Are you ready for some lunch?"

"Yes, definitely," JoJo replied.

They exchanged parting words with Alice, then Belinda and JoJo headed for home.

"Mom, I'm so tired," JoJo said. "I'm also relieved. Pastor Don said he wasn't targeting me. He said he would instead take me aside and talk to me privately, not from the pulpit."

"I can see you've had a momentous day," Belinda said. "I'm proud of you for asking, rather than staying angry."

"I learned we can think we know what is happening, and we can be mistaken," JoJo said. "I thought you told him all about me. Sorry, Mom."

They looked at each other, and laughed.

# 36
# PAYBACKS

*One person's rights stop where another person's rights begin.*

JoJo sat down at the table to finish her book report while the casserole heated up in the oven for lunch.

"Mom? How should I thank the band for all of those notes and the balloons and everything? I can't even put it into words how much it means to me."

"Hmmm. That's a good one. How many students are in the band?"

"More than 100, and most, if not all, wrote a note."

"I'll have to think about it," Belinda said, and walked into the other room.

*So much has happened since I wrote this book report the first time,* JoJo thought. *No, I don't want to put that personal stuff in it. I'm sticking with the book.*

About the time the casserole was ready to come out of the oven, JoJo's mother returned to the kitchen with a notebook and pencil in her hands.

"JoJo, what if we make cookies? I could make a double batch of heart-shaped cookies, like the soft ones we always make at Christmas, and a double batch of chocolate chip, and a full pan of brownies."

"That sounds so good. But don't you always rest on Sunday?" JoJo asked.

"Yes, and I do intend to take a nap before all of this," Belinda said.

"Good, because I was hoping to rest, too. I'm so exhausted. I can't believe I'm still struggling this much."

"Yes, healing takes time," Belinda said. "So let's eat, and then rest, and then we'll bake cookies. Have you thought about how to thank the Kite Club? Do you know when their next meeting is?"

"For starters, I plan on writing a thank you note," JoJo said. "Then when my arm is better, I want to make some Friend Kites for them to give away. I think that is so beautiful."

# 37
# PREPARATIONS

*Make mistakes and learn from them, then try again.*

JoJo ate her lunch quietly, thinking about what adds up to a mountain of kindnesses within a few days. Even the casserole, her protein shake and the cardamom cookies were given as acts of love.

"Thank you, Mom," she said, and carried her dishes to the sink.

"I'll get those today," Belinda said, so JoJo turned toward the stairs, grateful as the discomfort had increased. She hoped the medicine would ease the ache from the bruises as she hauled herself up the steps and into her room.

As JoJo snuggled into bed, she pulled Alice's Bible onto Rory so she could reread the passage the pastor talked about, God's list for dealing with enemies: love, do good, bless, pray.

When JoJo awoke, the Bible was closed on her nightstand, and she clutched Rory close to her, like she used to when she was little.

The dream she remembered was of her dad, pushing her high in a swing he cut from an old tire and hung with rope from a huge maple tree in their yard. She giggled and giggled, safe in her tire swing, safe with her daddy.

No matter how high he pushed, she felt safe.

*I have to go back to school tomorrow,* JoJo thought. She stared at the ceiling.

"God, how can I go back to school?" she prayed, quietly. A tear rolled onto her pillow, then another.

Pulling a note card and a pen from her nightstand drawer, JoJo began writing names of people she intended to pray for, like the pastor said, but she did not start with her enemies. First on her list was her mom, then Alice, Rosemary, Julie, Sharon, the Sunday school class, Mr. Schoolcraft, the pastor and her teachers. For enemies, the only three she could come up with were Amanda, the locker stacker, and the foot.

"I'll start praying there," JoJo said. "God, what does it mean to love my enemies?"

After she told God how she felt about the events of the past few days and she prayed forgiveness over her enemies, JoJo cried more. Then, aroused by an aroma of fresh baked cookies, she made her way downstairs to the kitchen.

"Mom, you didn't wait for me?" JoJo asked, astonished at everything her mother accomplished. "I thought you were going to take a nap, too."

"I did, JoJo. You slept for hours, and you probably needed it. Besides, most of what needed to be done required two hands. I could use some help icing the heart cookies, if you think you can spread icing with one hand. If not, it's okay. I can do it."

"I think I can," JoJo said, looking across the table full of cookies while her mother chose sprinkles.

JoJo swirled thin white icing with a spatula, and smoothed it on top of a cookie farthest from the pan. Her mother picked it up, added sprinkles over a bowl, and set the cookie on a pan to dry.

"This is working," JoJo said.

"Indeed," Belinda said. They looked at each other and smiled.

"These will be a delicious thank you," JoJo said.

Within half an hour the whole batch of large soft cookies was decorated, waiting for the icing to set up.

"Good work," Belinda said. "Are you hungry?"

"I shouldn't be after how much I slept," JoJo said, "But, yeah."

They settled on simple salads of lettuce, spinach, green pepper chunks, shredded carrots and cheese, followed by barbecue cheeseburgers on multi-grain buns.

They worked together to clean up the remaining baking and supper dishes.

"Mom, do you want to play Skeeter Scratch?" JoJo asked.

"Sure. We haven't played that in a long time," her mother said.

"Since before we moved here," JoJo said, retrieving the box of wooden tiles with two sets of dots on the same side of each one from a shelf in a hall closet.

She watched her mother wash the table again, then dry it to ensure it was free from stray drips of cookie frosting. Then JoJo laid out the tiles face down in the middle while her mother picked up a pen and paper and wrote down their names at the top.

They chose seven tiles each, and her mother came up with the double nine tile, which always started the action.

"Let the game begin," JoJo said, laughing in anticipation, because the family version is played quickly.

JoJo and Belinda slapped tiles onto the table, beginning with the nines until the double tile was filled. Then they worked to fill other double tiles as they were laid down. Belinda hardly had time to write the scores down between rounds. JoJo's bad arm, causing her to play one handed, hampered her style of selecting tiles for first, second or third plays, but she played fast anyway.

After the last round, Belinda looked at her and said, "JoJo, you won."

"But you let me win."

"Never!"

They looked at each other, smiling, tired but thankful for the diversion of a fun time.

"How about your putting away the tiles while I clean the table again and we platter the cookies so they will be ready for tomorrow?" Belinda said. "I have three platters and they just might hold all of the cookies. I would like the platters back, though."

Belinda pretended to be surprised when one of the tender cookies broke in half. She handed one half to JoJo for a taste test.

"Worth the effort?" Belinda asked.

"Up to our highly held family standards," JoJo said, pretending to talk like her father.

*No family is perfect,* JoJo thought, *but ours has a lot of good times together.*

Belinda used the brownies to establish a pattern on each of the platters, then they filled in with the chocolate chip and heart-shaped cookies. Each platter presented a different theme, to add interest, Belinda explained. They covered them with wrap and set each platter in a box to stabilize them for the trip to school in the morning.

With the work done, JoJo's mother looked at her and paused.

"JoJo, what do you want to happen at school tomorrow morning?" Belinda asked.

"I've been thinking about that all weekend," JoJo replied. "I don't want kids to get in trouble, exactly, but I do want the dirty tricks to stop, and I want to talk this over with them. I want to talk it out for real, not just for a wimpy, 'Sorry,' and back to business as usual. I want to talk it out and I want things to change. I don't want other kids to be targeted like I have been."

"Whoa, how are you going to accomplish all of this?" her mother said. "That's a pretty tall order."

"Just talking to the principal isn't going to make a big enough change," JoJo said. "I think it has to come from us kids. I think we need to change how we treat each other. If the school could figure this out, they probably would have done it a long time ago."

"Um, you're just starting to get a little better," Belinda said. "I don't want you to take on too much, too soon."

"Mom, when I woke up I almost panicked. I'm scared to go back," JoJo said. "But I have to walk through this. I'm going to make a difference in my school, with my classmates.

"I've been wondering... Why didn't anyone from band be my friend? I met some of them at band camp, and that was before school started. Amanda wasn't even around yet. Are other kids as lonely as I have been? If it weren't for you and Mrs. Stacey and Rosemary and Julie, I don't think I could have made it this far. I have support at home."

"That's true," Belinda said.

"Why was my other school so friendly, and this school is so scary," JoJo asked, "and cold?"

"Well, your dad and his friends had something to do with that," Belinda said. "Your dad went to your old school. He and his good friends were in a biology class, and an upperclassman, a girl, took the same class. She was assigned a boy in your dad's class as a lab partner, so she was talking to him. Your dad and his friends challenged her, 'How come you're talking to him?' It was as if the boy wasn't goon enough for her, or something. She looked at them and said, 'Why not?' They decided, and convinced the other classmates, that from then on there were no more cliques. Everybody should be good enough to talk to everybody else."

"Dad did that?" JoJo said in astonishment.

"That's one of the reasons I married him," Belinda said. "It changed the whole school. That school is still friendly. Most students don't want their school to be a war zone."

"That's for sure," JoJo said. "But I can't do this alone. Mom, can we pray about this?"

"Sure. You start."

"Dear God, we come to you asking for your help," JoJo prayed. "How do you want my school to be? Please give me wisdom, to know who to talk to and who to trust and how to go about changing my school into a positive place for everyone. God, this isn't too big for you. You're God. You created all of the stars and planets and hung them in place. You created every living thing, too. Wow! Please help my school. Show me and Mom what to do. She has seen change happen before in school. I want to see it happen now. I'm yours, God. I love you. In Jesus' name, amen."

# 38
# FACE IT



The morning was chilly with a fresh dusting of frost on the grass and fall flowers. JoJo awoke before her alarm to a startling feeling of dread, then realized it was because of going back to school and facing all of the students, and the unknown.

*Will I be safe?* JoJo wondered. *I just don't know.*

She could hear her mother's voice downstairs, talking to her boss from work, saying she would be in after she drops JoJo off at school and she talks to the principal.

*Well, Mom isn't planning on a long, drawn out conversation,* JoJo thought. *Maybe I shouldn't, either. Maybe the first introduction of my idea should be short. We can build on it later.*

"God, please guide me, and protect me and all of the other kids," JoJo prayed. She asked God to bless the people whose names she wrote on the list the day before, and to forgive Amanda, the locker stacker and the foot. She read another Psalm, and worked toward getting ready for school.

Her mother carried out the cookies before JoJo made it downstairs for breakfast.

They looked into each others' eyes, and though the kind gestures were genuine, JoJo could tell her mother was feeling the same way about the morning and the visit with the principal.

JoJo breathed out the tension, and settled on walking with God and her mother into that building. She wasn't going alone. Not this time.

They checked JoJo's arm together, and even though the swelling was not as noticeable in her hand, her elbow and lower arm were still very sore and tender, and the movement had not yet returned.

"How can we protect this, so you won't be hurt if someone accidentally bumps you?" Belinda asked. "Wait. I have that muff my mom made for me. What if we cover your sorest spots with the muff? Would that be okay?"

"Can I wear Dad's sweatshirt over it?" JoJo asked, thinking of other big, warm shirts of his than the one she already wore.

"Yes," Belinda said. JoJo pulled the muff over her elbow. Belinda helped JoJo into the sweatshirt, and placed her coat over top of her shoulders, securing it at the neck.

"It is very chilly out this morning," Belinda said. "You may not need the coat later. Mrs. Stacey will bring you home again this afternoon, but you may need to stay in her room until she is done tutoring."

"That's no problem," JoJo said, thankful for a ride.

Belinda carried JoJo's books and trumpet out to the car, and they both got in for the ride to school.

"Here goes," JoJo said.

# 39

# PRINCIPAL

If it's hard walk through it and look up.


Only the first bus and some teachers had arrived before JoJo and Belinda pulled into a parking space at the school.

"Mom, maybe we can get this taken care of soon," JoJo said.

"I hope so. Let's pray," Belinda said. "Loving Heavenly Father, our protector and guide, our joy and strength. We ask you to go before us and with us into this school, and everywhere we need to go today. Guide our conversations and our understandings. Lead us, Lord, our Good Shepherd. We know you care about everyone in this school, so we ask for your best outcomes for these troubles. And give us your wisdom. Thank you so much! In Jesus' name, amen.

"Are you ready?" Belinda asked.

"Ready. With God on our side, no one else stands a chance."

"Um, logistics," Belinda said. "Principal first, books and trumpet next, cookies last."

"Let's go," JoJo said, eager to clear the first challenge.

They walked up to the door of the school, pulled the handle, and the door was locked.

"What gives?" Belinda asked.

"We still have five minutes before the doors open," JoJo said, peering in at a clock on the wall.

Her mother knocked as the principal rounded a corner of the hallway. She held up her hands in a questioning gesture.

"Mr. Ferres," she said as he opened the door a crack. "We need to talk to you about things that happened Friday."

"Come in," he said, and showed them to his small but tidy office. They sat down.

"What can I do for you?" he asked.

Belinda introduced herself and JoJo to the principal, and explained about the events leading to JoJo's fall at the pep assembly.

"Quiet frankly, I did not want to send my daughter back after I heard how she has struggled, and then this turned physical, too," Belinda said, quietly and respectfully. "Can you help us?"

Mr. Ferres turned to JoJo and asked, "Can you help me with names of students you are having trouble with?"

"The only name I know right now is Amanda," JoJo said. "I've tried to be a friend, but she always seems to be saying something snarky or mean. And I don't know who stacked my locker, and I don't know whose foot tripped me, or even if it was on purpose. I don't know. It may have been an accident. But I've been afraid to come back to school, and I'm not usually like that."

"We did have some people report what they saw on Friday, but some of them did not know your name, JoJo." Mr. Ferres said. "I'll ask around and see what I can find out."

"The band did some beautiful things for JoJo on Saturday," Belinda said. "And so did the Kite Club. I don't know if you know about them."

"Yes, they're involved in the school," Mr. Ferres said.

"We made cookies for the band. I have them in the car. They're in three big boxes. Is there anyone who can help us take them to the band room?" Belinda asked.

"Yes, the director usually has aides. I'll call down and see if they can bring a cart for the cookies," Mr. Ferres said. "And JoJo, several students already volunteered to help you carry books or whatever between classes. Do you know a girl named Sharon? She's new, too. And there are two boys."

JoJo and her mother looked at each other, and smiled.

# 40

## START

A cut rose lasts a few days; a rose bush lasts for years. They both mean love.

As JoJo and Belinda carried her books and trumpet to her locker, two boys pushed a cart up the hallway toward the school entry.

"Hi JoJo," one called to her. "Are you okay? We're sorry you got stepped on."

"Yeah," the other one said. "I was one of the ones who stepped on you. I'm sorry! Are you okay?"

"I'll be okay," JoJo said, feeling a little embarrassed, but glad for two more friendly voices and faces at school.

The boys followed her mother to the car for the boxes of cookies, while JoJo arranged her books in order for the school day. Meanwhile, Sharon walked by JoJo and opened her locker.

"Hi JoJo," Sharon said. "You're not usually here this early. How are you? I saw you fall."

"I'll be okay," JoJo said. "I'm sore. My arm doesn't work right, yet. I fell on my arm trying to protect my trumpet."

"I told the principal I would help you get to class and stuff," Sharon said.

135

"Thank you," JoJo said. "That makes all the difference."

"Did you hear what happened to Amanda?" Sharon said. "There was a big fight. It was her and her mom and her mom's boyfriend. Police went to the apartment and took Amanda away over the weekend."

"No, I didn't hear," JoJo said.

*I feel sad about that,* JoJo thought. *My home life has always been great. Well, except for the cancer. But none of us has a choice about that. No wonder I should pray for my enemies.*

JoJo and Sharon carried her things to their first class, American literature, and JoJo handed her rewritten book report to Mrs. Smith immediately.

"Thank you, JoJo," the teacher said. "How are you?"

"I'm sore. Thanks for asking. Nothing broken. That's the good thing," she said, trying to remain positive.

The girls walked into the hallway in time for JoJo's mother and the boys to return with the cart loaded with cookies. JoJo pulled her trumpet from her locker and walked with them to the band room.

"JoJo," Mr. McCluggage called loudly, "how are you?"

"I'll be okay," JoJo said, smiling. "Sore, and my arm doesn't work yet. But it's not broken. Thank you so much for everything the band did for me. It meant more than you could know. I was so surprised."

"Well, we care," Mr. McCluggage said. "You are one of us. You matter."

"Thank you," she said, thinking, *I'm so shocked. I shouldn't be, because of their kindness and reaching out, but it matters to hear him say that.*

"And I hear there are cookies?" Mr. McCluggage said. "The question is: Will there still be cookies by the end of the day?"

He grinned.

"I'm joking," he said. "There will be cookies for your band last period. Thank you for bringing them. They were totally unexpected, but all the more appreciated."

JoJo smiled at him, then placed her trumpet in the instrument room. She and Belinda thanked the boys and walked back up the hall, which was filling with students.

Belinda walked along JoJo's left side, to protect her as much as she could, then hugged her and said she would see her after work.

"Thanks, Mom," JoJo said. "I feel better already. Your coming with me, and the cookies, and everything. Thanks, Mom."

The girls at the corner of the two hallways did not seem quite the same without Amanda. JoJo and Sharon walked into the classroom and Belinda walked by the group without any problem.

*Second challenge handled, at least for the moment,* JoJo thought as she slid into her desk slowly. She felt the bruises on her back and legs even more while sitting in the hard desk.

Mrs. Smith called the class to attention and the private conversations stopped.

"Today you will be giving oral reports on the books you read and book reports you turned in on Friday," Mrs. Smith said. "JoJo, will you be first?"

JoJo smiled. She had forgotten about the oral book reports. But she got up and walked to the front of the class. Rather than show her nervousness, JoJo chose to look students in the eye and speak as if she were speaking to each one, which was something her father taught her.

She closed her report comparing what the character, Ginny, revealed about her experience of love, and what JoJo witnessed in her parents' relationship.

JoJo thanked Mrs. Smith, and sat down.

"Thank you, JoJo," Mrs. Smith said. "Brian, will you be next, please?"

About halfway through the class, Amanda burst through the doorway, shoved a pink late pass toward Mrs. Smith, twirled and sat down at her desk. She didn't even carry in any books, notebooks or pens.

Interrupted, the boy giving his report seemed startled. Mrs. Smith encouraged him, and he started his book report over at the beginning.

When he was finished, Mrs. Smith called Amanda to the front.

"Uh, book report?" Amanda stammered. Her nose was red, and it looked like she had been crying. "I forgot. I can't remember anything. I can't do this."

She sat back down.

"Please see me after class," Mrs. Smith said. "Robert, will you please come to the front for your report?"

As the other students presented reports, JoJo thought about Amanda.

*I do not feel good about bad things happening to her,* JoJo thought. *I guess, God, that is you working in me. I can't explain it any other way. I wonder what, if anything, I should say to Amanda.*

But at the end of the class, Sharon walked up to JoJo's desk to help carry books with other students filing past them, and Amanda walked up to Mrs. Smith's desk, so there was no chance for JoJo to talk to her.

*God, I'm leaving this in your hands,* JoJo prayed silently. *If you want me to say something to Amanda, please give me the words and the opportunity.*

# 41

# ALGEBRA

If you borrow something, give it back in as good of shape, or better than when you borrowed it.

By second period, JoJo was thankful for Sharon's help with her books and walking through the hallway.

*It makes all the difference having someone walk alongside me,* JoJo thought. *I don't feel nearly as alone and scared as before.*

She hoped Sharon was feeling good about it, too. But she couldn't tell.

*Sharon is so quiet,* JoJo thought, wondering how to get her to talk without feeling pushed into it.

After the hours of struggle over one algebra assignment, JoJo felt shocked when the class scored the homework problems together on the board, and she only missed one.

Not being able to concentrate and figure things out and pull herself out of the emotional pit felt scary. She didn't want to go there again, but she also could not tell if the struggle was over.

*I'm not going to heap a bunch of worry on top of today,* JoJo thought. *I'm just going to focus on one class at a time for now. That's enough.*

In Biology, Mr. Markel passed out the grasshoppers the students caught at the end of last week.

"They're dead," a boy said in a matter-of-fact voice.

JoJo and Sharon gazed at their grasshopper, legs curled in, dead.

"Yes, they're dead," Mr. Markel said. "They would not have survived the two hard frosts in a row this weekend. So we're using for science what nature was going to do to them, anyway. Take out your notebooks and write down everything you notice about your grasshopper. Use tweezers and carefully lift it from the jar. Grasshoppers have been around you ever since you were tiny children learning how to walk in the grass. But you never had the chance to really see them. They were moving too fast. You've been moving too fast. Slow down and notice your grasshopper."

JoJo measured the head and the thorax, and tried to measure the legs but they were stiff and she didn't want to break them.

Sharon noted the grasshopper was "grass green," then added, "But wait. There is a rusty brown color on his wings."

Sharon sketched the grasshopper's shape in pencil, then opened her set of colored pencils to document details she didn't notice on Friday.

"I'm getting into this," Sharon said.

JoJo noticed the shape of the feet and lower legs. They pulled a four-inch magnifying glass out of a lab table drawer and looked closer at the grasshopper.

"This is fascinating," JoJo said, and Sharon took a turn. She revised part of her drawing with closer details.

Mr. Markel looked at progress in each science notebook, and picked up Sharon's sketch.

"This is nice. Can you do this really big on the board?" he asked.

"I guess," Sharon answered, and shrugged.

"How about tomorrow," he said. "Good job on this."

"Thank you," she said.

After he walked away, Sharon turned to JoJo.

"I can't believe it," she said. "He is asking me to draw in front of the whole class."

JoJo grinned at her. "Well, if I can fall in front of the whole school and not die from embarrassment, you can draw your grasshopper."

They laughed.

"Seriously, Sharon. You did a really nice job of drawing our grasshopper," JoJo said. "You deserve recognition for it."

"I need to practice drawing it really big," Sharon said.

"Got any sidewalk chalk?" JoJo asked. "The whole town is your canvas."

Sharon tossed her head in laughter and said, "JoJo, we were meant to be friends."

# 42

# WORN OUT

*Who you honor matters.*

By the time they made it to the lunch room, JoJo was feeling tired and sore. But there was not time for a lengthy nap during the school day.

*It's okay,* she thought, *I'll just get through this the best I can.*

She opened her bag of cardamom cookies, removed one and handed the bag to Sharon.

"Thank you so much for your help," JoJo said. "I couldn't have made it through today without you."

"No problem at all," Sharon said. She brightened when she saw the cookies.

"So tell me about the Kite Club. Are you joining?" JoJo asked.

"My mom told me to try it for a few weeks before we make the decision," Sharon said. "I have my church youth group, and Mom wants me to visit my grandmother often since she hasn't been feeling well.

"But flying a kite is an experience like no other," Sharon explained. "You're in control, yet not in control at the same time. You're at the mercy of the way the wind blows, yet you can respond and change the outcome. So in a way flying kites has been freeing for me. I guess. I"m learning so much."

"The Friend Kite floored me," JoJo said. "I was struggling inside, feeling sore all over and kind of depressed. Okay, I was depressed. I couldn't think, and didn't care. It was scary. Then we found balloons and bears and a basket of notes the band left on my porch. Then my mom and I talked at the beach, and the Kite Club came and gave me a Friend Kite. It helped so much."

"I'm not allowed to tell you who tripped you," Sharon said.

"Why not?" JoJo asked.

"The principal told me not to tell," Sharon said. "They're investigating and I'm not allowed to tell anyone what I know."

JoJo felt confused, but glad there was an investigation, at least. She munched her peanut butter and honey sandwich quietly.

*I wish I could take a nap,* JoJo thought. She drank the protein drink her mother added to her lunch bag, and the girls headed to the next class.

JoJo struggled through until the end, but not very well. Exhaustion drained her ability to think. When she arrived at study hall, she asked to go to the nurse's office. But when JoJo looked inside, another student already stretched out on the couch, and it was Amanda.

JoJo trudged back to study hall, sat in her seat, laid her head on her good arm with her left hand in her lap, and fell asleep.

She felt a hand on her good shoulder.

"What is her name?" the study hall monitor said. "JoJo. JoJo. It's time to wake up and go to your next class."

Since Sharon was not in band and JoJo did not need her books in band, they parted and JoJo walked to the instrument room.

"Do you want me to open your case for you?" a boy offered.

"Yes, thanks," JoJo said.

"I'll carry your music," a girl said.

"Thank you," JoJo said, still sleepy but smiling.

As the students found their seats, Mr. McCluggage placed JoJo's note to the band on his director's music stand. He called JoJo over.

"JoJo, how are you feeling?"

"I can't use my left arm yet, and I'm really sore," she said.

"Will you be able to march by Friday?" he asked.

JoJo froze. *Oh, no! I hadn't thought that far ahead,* she thought. *I'm just trying to get through today.*

"I really don't know," she said. "I don't know what to say."

"What if we give you one more week to rest?" he said. "Practice with the band and come along with us. We'll march another student this Friday, and we'll talk again on Monday."

"Okay," JoJo said, feeling a sting of embarrassment, yet realizing another student needed to learn her spot in the show. Plus, as tired as she felt, she was grateful, too, for an extra week of healing.

"Thank you," he said. "I appreciate your leadership and musicianship. But we need to take care of you, too."

"Mr. McCluggage, this band is amazing," JoJo said. "The things left on our porch really helped. I appreciate it so much."

"You're welcome. And please don't get in the way when we put out the cookies," he said. "No offense, but I don't want you to get trampled."

She laughed with him, and went to her seat.

Most of what JoJo needed to do during band, playing her trumpet, she did with her right hand. It felt awkward, but she enjoyed playing with her section. Toward the end of the period, Mr. McCluggage called the names of six boys, who carried in three tables, and three more boys who each carried in a platter of cookies.

Always the showman, Mr. McCluggage announced: "Ladies and Gentlemen, before you lies evidence, in beauty and great delight to all, of the thankfulness of JoJo and her mother for your thoughtfulness last weekend. Two cookies each. You may partake."

In her heart JoJo savored their responses, and wished her mother were there to enjoy the moment.

# 43

# TRUMPETER

A kindness takes a moment, but it could change a life.

While the band headed for the practice field, Mr. Mc-Cluggage spoke in the hallway with the football coach, sealing a deal. The coach called aside a player, whose back was turned to the band. JoJo saw his head move up and down, then the player took off his helmet and headed for the band practice field.

*Herman?* JoJo thought. *What's going on?*

Herman reported to Mr. McCluggage, by then at the sidelines holding his megaphone. They spoke, and Herman trotted over to where JoJo was lined up with her section.

"I'm supposed to shadow you," Herman said.

"You are?" JoJo asked, astonished.

"Yeah, I play trumpet," Herman said. "I'm just on the football team for fall. Coach says I can help out the band until you feel better. He said we should all work together."

"Oh," JoJo said. "Thanks."

Mr. McCluggage said I don't need to play trumpet today. I didn't bring it anyway. You can play if you feel up to it. That way I can hear the part along with shadowing you in the marching. He will take care of getting me the music and the drill instructions for tomorrow."

"Okay," JoJo said. "Would it be okay if you stand on my right side?"

"I don't see why not," he said.

Again, JoJo was looking into those soft brown eyes. *I wonder what that expression means,* she thought. She shrugged it off. *I need to teach the drill to my shadow, and I intend to do a great job of it.*

# 44

# RIDE HOME

Always ask: How can I help?


An hour later, JoJo stood at Mrs. Stacey's door with two books clutched in her right arm and her coat wedged in the crook of her left arm.

Two younger students sat on either side of their reading teacher, listening to her dramatic voice changes as she read one of her favorite classic tales.

JoJo enjoyed the moment, sensing Mr. Stacey provided more than simple tutoring for strugglers, just like she reached out to JoJo when she needed help.

When the tale wound around into a happy ending, Mrs. Stacey closed the book and hugged the students close. The little boys reached up and kissed her on her cheeks, then found their books and coats and headed for the door.

Mrs. Stacey chuckled.

"Are you ready, JoJo? she asked. "I'll just be a minute."

The two walked side-by-side down the hallway, recounting the amazing parts of their day.

"Your mother asked if I knew of any good Christian counselors," Mrs. Stacey said. "I do know of one. She was going to call her to see if she has any availability. I'm glad more positive things opened up for you."

"I'm still shocked by the difference a few days have made," JoJo said, "and so thankful."

After Alice dropped her off, JoJo set her books on a chair on the porch, unlocked the front door and swung it open. She picked up the books and placed them on the dining room table, then shut the front door and headed upstairs.

*I can't keep going right now. I need rest.*

# 45
# OPENING

If you're not reading, you're not thinking.

JoJo sank into her soft pillow as if she were a bucket of lead dropping to the bottom of the ocean at high tide.

Overwhelmed, exhausted, thankful she made it through the day, somewhat.

*But I needed that nap in study hall,* she thought.

As she turned onto her good side and stretched out, her soreness was engulfed in numbed exhaustion.

*Am I too tired to sleep?* JoJo thought. She yawned, and allowed relaxation to take over as she recounted kindnesses at school.

Somewhere far away she heard a key turn in a lock, a door groan open. A distant voice called gently, "JoJo, JoJo Darling..."

The voice didn't fit the dream, the band dream about trumpets playing jazz in the middle of the football game instead of football players marching the ball down the field.

"JoJo," the soft voice was beside her. She felt a hand on her shoulder. "Darling, are you okay? How are you feeling?"

"Mom?" JoJo opened her eyes. "Mom. Did you get off work early?"

"No," Belinda said, reaching down to her, then standing up. "I left a note in the kitchen. You didn't call me. I was so worried. Are you okay?"

"Oh, Mom. I'm sorry! I was so tired I didn't even go into the kitchen. Alice dropped me off and I went straight upstairs. I even fell asleep during study hall. And in band I had to train my replacement for Friday. It's Herman!"

Her mother paused, then said, "Well, there was a cancellation at the counselor's office for today at seven o'clock. If we hurry we can get you some supper and make the appointment on time. We don't want to be late since the counselor went above and beyond to take us.

"After today, we might be able to join group therapy, where we would just go paint in the group and then take the painting to a counselor to talk about privately. How does that sound?" Belinda asked. She waited.

"I think I need it. I need something," JoJo said. "Let's go. Can we pray?"

JoJo sat up in bed, and her mother sat beside her.

"Loving God, you brought us this far, and we're trusting you for the rest of the way," JoJo prayed. "Thank you for the beautiful things you have been doing. Please guide us and the counselor. I don't know what to say."

"Heavenly Father, yours is the glory," Belinda prayed. "We want to honor you. We need your help. Please wrap JoJo and the counselor in your loving arms, and guide the session and fill them with wisdom for reaching the inmost places that need your healing. And thank you for all you have done. We love you. In Jesus' name we pray, amen."

Belinda reached over and tousled JoJo's hair.

"Wash your face and freshen up a bit," she said. "I'll go down and fix supper."

*I'm so stiff and sore,* JoJo thought as she slowly stood up and walked to the bathroom, trying not to limp. *Just take normal steps.*

As she rounded the doorway into the kitchen, the sandwiches were prepared on plates and drinks were poured.

"Mom, that looks so good."

They sat down and prayed over the meal. Then munched and chatted about the day.

"You should have seen their faces when the boys brought out the cookies!" JoJo said. They looked at each other and smiled.

# 46

# ART THERAPY

*Take the trail where it leads you.*

*I feel nervous,* JoJo thought, as she and her mother entered the waiting room at the counselor's studio. A few minutes early, they sat down and waited for someone to acknowledge them.

JoJo heard an unfamiliar woman's voice say, "You did great work today. I'm proud of you. It may not feel good for some time. That's normal. And be gentle with yourself. This is like surgery. We opened a wound. It needs time to heal correctly. Are you available for next week?"

She heard the sound of a door closing, then footsteps down a tiled hallway, then a woman in her 50s appeared in the waiting room.

"Hello, Belinda!" the woman said. "You must be JoJo. I'm so glad to meet you. My name is Abigail Thatcher, I go by Gail. And I told your mother, I'm licensed to do art therapy in this state. I used to be an art teacher until I went through some very bad stuff, and it was my art that pulled me through to healing and moving on. Some things we don't have words for. The art helps draw that out in a different language, a visual language.

"And you don't need to be an artist to do art therapy," Gail said. "I won't be asking you to paint a building or a bird or a banana. Here we use colors to paint emotions. Sometimes as we paint, an image or clue emerges. If so, we follow that. We go with it. Are you ready to get started?"

JoJo and Belinda looked at each other, smiled in a tense, nervous way, and nodded.

"Good, follow me, please," Gail said. "Here are smocks, one for each of you. Belinda, you will be going into a room next door so each of you can do the work you need to do. This is very intensely personal. At the end of the session, you may not be 'done,' so I have this rack for paintings to dry. No one is allowed to look at others' paintings. These are not for display. I write your first names or a nickname on your painting and turn the rack so no one can look at yours, either. But even if they did, they could not understand it."

Gail smiled at them as they pulled on the smocks and rolled up the sleeves.

The acrylic paint dries quickly," she said, "but the paintings probably will not be completely dry by the end of the session. Another person is scheduled to arrive in an hour, so that is when this session will end.

"You might be surprised how intense an hour can be here," Gail said. She turned to JoJo and said, "While I show your mother to the other room, please choose any color and make a mark on the canvas anywhere."

As they walked out, JoJo selected an intense blue, and dabbed a splotch in an upper area of the white canvas. Gail returned.

"JoJo, your mother told me you are a Christian, and you have been seeking God about things going on in your life," she said. JoJo nodded. "And that's good to know, because there are people who sit in churches who are not Christian. I would work with them differently. So since you already are seeking God on your own, please continue to seek him during your session. Please pray and ask God to guide you as you open up your heart for healing."

Gail waited while JoJo closed her eyes for a few minutes, opened them and smiled.

"Thank you. Now, remember when I said we paint emotions? Select any colors you want and paint emotions with them. I will not tell you how or what to paint, and I will not suggest colors. And you're painting from your heart not your head, so don't think about it. Just paint."

With those instructions, Gail turned and walked to an office area, visible to JoJo through a window. She walked into the studio again.

"By the way, do you see the chair beside you?" Gail asked. "That is just in case you need to sit down."

JoJo thanked her, and splotched more and more blue on the big rectangle canvas. *I like blue,* she thought. She selected purple paint, and stroked long diagonal stripes through the blue, lining them up alongside each other, parallel.

*Painting feels good, just adding colors,* JoJo thought. She added splotches of red, yellow, green, orange, blue and purple in a curving line.

Then JoJo selected tan paint, and pushed upward on the brush, making short upward strokes. She added some smooth strokes, but not wiping out all of the blue. *Kind of whispy,* JoJo thought. She stepped back, and what emerged from the canvas evoked immediate, rib-racking sobs in wave after wave.

JoJo could hardly breathe. She tried to hide behind the canvas so Gail would not see, and sobbed so forcefully it rocked her body. She felt for the chair and sat down, still sobbing.

*God help,* she prayed silently, unable to speak. She caught her breath and sobbed some more. Unintentionally some moans escaped from deep within her. Her whole body shook. *I can't stop,* she thought, and somehow she knew she mustn't stop. *God help,* she prayed, over and over. Gradually, the sobbing eased up. She started to breathe more regularly. *My stomach is sore from bawling. My lungs hurt, too. But something is different, I can feel it. Something is different in me.*

As JoJo looked at the painting, Gail walked over to her.

"What is happening? How are you doing?" Gail asked gently. "Are you okay? You can tell me about this if you want to, but you don't have to tell me. It's up to you."

"It's Dad," JoJo said, smiling through tears. "It's Dad and the Friend Kite. Dad was watching me with the Friend Kite."

The crying started again, not as forceful as before. JoJo sat down. She tried to look up at Gail and smile.

Gail looked at the painting, looked at JoJo and nodded. She smiled kindly, and JoJo knew she understood, even though the splotches of paint did not really look like a person at this point. *But it's what it means to me,* JoJo thought.

"This art therapy can wear a person out," JoJo said. Gail smiled, and placed a hand on her shoulder.

"You did good work today," Gail said. "It's because you were seeking God in it, and you were ready. You needed to grieve, didn't you?"

JoJo nodded.

"It may not happen like this every time, and that's okay," Gail said. "Trust God and your heart. You made huge strides toward healing today."

"I've been holding it in," JoJo said. "I didn't want to hurt my mom."

"That's what brave ones do, and it costs you dearly," Gail said. "It's okay to let it out now. And your mom knows you need to. She's on your side in this."

JoJo turned back to the canvas.

"Is there still time to paint?" she asked.

"Just a few minutes," Gail said. "Then it's time to clean up. I'm going to see how your mom is doing."

As Gail walked out of the room, JoJo turned to the canvas but could not paint on it again, not just yet. She felt exhausted in a good way. She swirled the paint brush in a jar of water and stood it up in another jar beside it, the way she had found it.

"Dad," she said, and cried some more, quietly.

# 47

# JESUS EVERY DAY

Wear your Bible out, reading it.


When Belinda walked into the studio, JoJo could tell she had been crying, too.

"I'll put the paintings away with your first names on them, so they will be here for next time," Gail was saying. "You both opened up pretty quickly, which is good. But there's no pressure on the next session. It may go a different way next time, and that's okay."

"Thank you so much," Belinda said. She looked at JoJo and smiled. "Are you ready to go home?"

JoJo handed the smock to Gail.

Mom and daughter walked out of the building with JoJo's good arm around her mom, and her mother's hand on JoJo's left shoulder.

"I needed this really bad," JoJo said. "Thanks, Mom."

"We need to thank Alice," Belinda said. "She paid for our first five sessions. She said she had been thinking about it for a couple of months, and wanted to make sure we were ready."

"Mom, what is it about Alice?" JoJo asked. "How does she always seem to know what to do for people, and when? I mean, she just shows up for so many people."

"I asked her the same thing, and she told me a long time ago she decided to make Jesus her Lord in everyday life," Belinda said. "Every day and every day. And the closer you get to Jesus, the more you see and understand. And Jesus guides you."

"So she's living her faith..." JoJo said. "I want faith like that."

The ride in the car was quiet at first.

"Mom, how did your session go?" JoJo asked. "I mean, you don't have to tell me."

"It's okay," Belinda said. "When I first started painting, I dabbled a little yellow, that's one of my happy colors, yellow, just to get started. I added some around, here and there. 'Oh, sunshine,' I thought. Then I added some gold and some orange. Then I got really brave and made a messy blob of brown, then more brown blobs. And I broke down and cried."

Belinda blinked back tears as she drove.

"Mom, do you need to pull over?" JoJo asked. "Here's a park. We can pull over and talk."

"Good idea," Belinda said, as she swung the car into the parking lot. "Do you feel like walking and talking? Or just talking?"

"This time, just talking is good enough," JoJo said.

"I didn't want to dump this on you," Belinda said.

"What do you mean? We're close. It's okay," JoJo said.

Belinda looked into her eyes, and paused.

"It was me as a scaredy cat lion," she said.

"What? You? You're the bravest person I know," JoJo said. "I admire you so much. 'Scaredy cat' is never a phrase I would connect with you."

"But it's how I feel," Belinda said.

"Oh, that's right. I'm sorry," JoJo said, then sat quietly.

"It's not easy being a mom and a dad," Belinda said.

"You do a great job," JoJo said, as they looked into each other's tearful eyes. Her mother smiled sadly and looked down at her hands in her lap beneath the steering wheel. "Do you want to hear about mine?"

"That's up to you," Belinda said. "I was warned not to ask and not to pry."

"You're not like that," JoJo said. "My first blobs were blue, because I like blue. So I was making blue blobs all over, then some parallel purple lines, then different colors, and tan. I was happy, just adding colors and adding colors, then I stepped back and looked at it. It was Dad. Dad and the Friend Kite."

JoJo shook her head. She sighed.

"I had no clue what I was painting," she said. "When it hit me, I just started sobbing and sobbing so hard. And it doesn't even look like dad, or the Friend Kite. It's just what it means to me. Anyone else could look at it and not know, at least at this point. I tried to paint more, but couldn't."

Sounds like we both needed to grieve," Belinda said. "We've been trying so hard to be brave and strong. We needed to let go of it and let it out. Still, I'm glad we chose not to attack each other or do something negative and harmful. Can we work through this and still treat each other well, with respect?"

"That's how I want it," JoJo said. "I think we did that part right so far."

Belinda started the car and eased it onto the roadway for the remaining blocks home.

"This therapy is okay and everything, but I'm exhausted," JoJo said, as Belinda turned the car into the driveway.

"Do you have homework?" Belinda asked.

"Some. I'll get it done quickly, then head for bed," JoJo said.

"I'm going to call Alice," Belinda said. "Don't worry. I'm not going to tell her about your painting. That's for you to tell, or not tell. It's up to you. I am going to thank her and tell her about mine. I think she might understand."

# 48

# GOD'S HEART

A spark starts a fire.

On Tuesday morning JoJo awakened gently to the song of a small black and white bird hopping among the branches of the cedar trees outside her window.

"Chicka-dee-dee-dee," the bird sang, over and over.

She stretched and reached for Alice's Bible on the night-stand beside her.

It opened to John 3. JoJo read about a Jewish teacher, Nicodemus, who visited Jesus at night "because he didn't want people to know," Alice had written in the margin.

"Am I like that?" JoJo asked herself, hoping it wasn't true. She read on, and came to a familiar verse, John 3:16. "For God so loved the world that he gave his one and only Son..."

*I can't imagine a love that big,* JoJo thought. *I don't think I could give up my child for the world.*

She read the next verse: "For God did not send his Son into the world to condemn the world, but to save the world through him."

*That's God's heart,* JoJo thought. *That's a big glimpse into the heart of God. He's a loving God. He wants us to be saved. He made the way.*

This time, when JoJo brought her hands together in prayer, it changed from being a duty or a rule to follow.

*It's a love thing,* JoJo thought. *Prayer is all about love. God is love, and when I come to him, I am showing love to him, because I want a relationship with him, too. I want to be close to him.*

"Loving Heavenly Father," JoJo said. "Thank you for wanting a relationship with me. Thank you for providing a way. I love you. I just read in your word, you love me, too. Thank you. I never need to feel lonely. You're near me. Thank you. In Jesus' name, amen."

As JoJo stood up and started selecting her clothes for school, her mother looked into the room.

"How is your arm feeling?"

"The swelling is starting to go down," JoJo said. "I'm still really sore, and I can't quite move it yet. My hand can move a little bit more."

"I forgot to tell you last night. Alice is going to pick you up for school so you don't have to walk and carry everything. I need to go to work a little early for a meeting and can't be late. My boss is going out of town. I packed your lunch, and added a protein drink, along with some juice."

"Thanks, Mom," JoJo said.

"And your breakfast is ready," Belinda said. "Bye-bye, Darling. I love you. Have a great day at school."

"Bye, Mom, love you!" JoJo said.

They looked at each other and smiled, then her mother turned and walked down the stairs and out the door.

*"God so loved the world that he gave...,"* JoJo thought, as she headed for the shower.

JoJo figured out how to hold the washcloth in her sore left hand while she squirted it with soap, and then transfer the washcloth to her right hand to scrub. She also figured out it was easier to wash her hair than try to keep it from getting wet.

She finished as quickly as possible, dressed, picked out her hair and headed downstairs for breakfast. There she realized something.

*Mom is always doing nice little things to show she loves me. I'm going to do things for her. I'm going to make a list.*

JoJo was waiting by the door with her jacket on when Alice parked her car in the driveway. She scooped her books into her good arm, grabbed her lunch bag in her left and walked out the door, being sure it locked behind her.

*I'm ready for a good day,* JoJo thought, smiling.

# 49
# FRUIT ON THE VINES

*What does God want you to do with your life? Did you ask?*

Alice opened the car door and JoJo sat down while holding her belongings.

As Alice sat in the driver's seat, JoJo thanked her for the art therapy sessions.

"I'm still in shock about what happened last night," JoJo said. "I had no clue about what I was painting then it hit me. I was painting my dad and the Friend Kite. I cried and cried."

Alice listened with a slight smile. She nodded. She started the car.

"Doing the work of inner healing is never easy," Alice said eventually, "but it's very worthwhile. In the end, there is good fruit on the vines."

"What a beautiful way to put it," JoJo said. "I do feel different after all that. But I'm not done yet, am I?"

"It takes some time," Alice said. "God knows how much you can handle. Trust him."

As they walked into the school building and down the long hallway toward Alice's classroom, JoJo realized she had forgotten to wear the muff on her arm for protection. The hall was nearly empty at the time, because students had not arrived yet.

*I'll be okay,* she thought. *I'll just have to be careful.*

She thanked Alice for the ride and walked to her locker. But as JoJo turned the corner, she saw several girls trying to open her locker door. She walked up behind them.

"Excuse me?" JoJo said. "Is there a problem here?"

They looked up. It was Amanda and two of her friends.

"Oh, it's you," Amanda said with a sneer.

"What's going on?" JoJo asked. "That's my locker."

"Oh, my mistake," Amanda said in a mocking voice. "Must be why it wouldn't open. C'mon, let's go."

They walked to the spot where their group usually stands in the morning, and looked at JoJo.

*You were caught in the act,* JoJo thought as she looked back at them. *I really don't feel like trying to catch another avalanche of books.*

JoJo bent down and laid her books and lunch on the floor, then stood up to try her locker combination. It turned. She opened her locker slowly. Nothing fell out.

*Good, they hadn't stacked it yet, or whatever they were going to do.*

JoJo sighed.

*While I'm dealing with the negative emotions inside me, I need someone to deal with Amanda. God help!*

She mentally ran through the order of her Tuesday classes so she could organize her books. In the meantime, Sharon walked by and greeted her.

"How are you feeling?" Sharon asked.

"Some better, but I forgot the muff I was wearing on my arm yesterday," JoJo said quietly so the girls wouldn't hear. "I feel so unprotected."

JoJo and Sharon laughed.

"Seriously, I am really sore," JoJo said. "But some good things happened last night, so I'm upbeat at the same time. Does that make sense?"

"What happened?" Sharon asked.

"My mom and I went to art therapy, and I started happily painting this picture with all of these colors, then I realized what it was supposed to be and bawled like a baby," JoJo explained.

"Art therapy? Did you go to Gail?" Sharon asked.

"Yes, Gail. She was so nice," JoJo said. "And it made all the difference. I can't even explain how I feel, other than it's different, in a good way."

"That's a fact. Gail has helped me so much, too," Sharon said. "Did you see my grasshoppers?"

"What?"

"You told me to get chalk and draw grasshoppers all over town, so I did," Sharon said. "It felt naughty at first, like I was going to get arrested or something. But then little kids started riding their bikes past me and saying, 'Oh cool.'"

They laughed.

"So you're ready for science lab now?"

"Somewhat," Sharon said. "And Mom said it doesn't have to look like the picture in the book. It just needs to look 'rather grasshoppery.' I can do that."

JoJo bent down to pick up her books, one at a time, and Sharon helped her.

"Don't turn around and look," Sharon said in a whisper, "but they have been glaring at us the entire time."

"The girls?" JoJo asked, also whispering.

"Yes," Sharon said.

"But why?" JoJo asked. "They act as if I've been doing things against them. But when I got here they were trying to get my locker open. It was Amanda and two others."

"Interesting," Sharon said. "Is it okay if we stick together again, today?"

"Yes, I'd be happy for some help," JoJo said. "Should I tell? I mean, they didn't actually get into my locker, that I know of. At least it wasn't stacked this time."

"I don't know," Sharon said.

"Let's just go to class before the hallway gets too crowded," JoJo said, pulling down her English grammar book and notebook. "If I find something wrong or missing, then I can go to the principal. I met him. I feel like he would help."

After the girls found their desks in the classroom, Sharon walked up to JoJo.

"You know, I was thinking," Sharon said. "I had a sprained ankle once, and the gym teacher wrapped it with this long stretchy bandage. Maybe the gym teacher or someone could wrap your elbow just for today at school, to protect it."

"That might work," JoJo said.

"Stay here. I'll go ask," Sharon said. She returned minutes later with the football coach, who wrapped JoJo's arm.

"How is it feeling?" he asked. "That's a nasty bruise. Can you do me a favor? Just take this off -- it comes unhooked like this -- just take it off and roll it up and give it to Herman when he comes to football practice. Can you do that for me?"

"Yes, thank you," JoJo said.

"And it's not supposed to be too tight," he said. "Your hand should not get numb or anything. If it does, come see me."

"Okay, thanks," JoJo said.

He left as other students began entering the classroom. JoJo turned around and thanked Sharon, then she sat down in her seat.

*Dear God,* JoJo prayed silently at her desk. *Thank you for good people who think up kind things to do for others. And thank you for foiling Amanda's plan. I'm supposed to pray for my enemies, so I ask you for good things to happen for Amanda, too. That you would bless her, and that she would know Jesus. Thank you, God. In Jesus' name, amen. And God, thank you for Sharon and the coach.*

# 50

# DIG FOR MORE

Pull weeds when they're little.

Having her arm wrapped felt very different to JoJo as she listened to teachers in grammar and algebra. The bandage was tight enough so that she knew it was there, but loose enough that it didn't seem to be causing swelling or added pain.

*It's just... different,* JoJo thought, *a distraction, and hopefully a protection.*

As she and Sharon walked together, they started talking a little more, and finding out about each other.

They were chatting while walking through the hall on the way to biology when suddenly five huge boys came barreling across the hallway backwards at them. The girls shrieked and stepped back as quickly as they could to avoid being smashed. The boys hit the wall of lockers just in front of the girls, then turned and looked at them, laughed and walked away.

"That was close," JoJo said. "I feel like my heart is in my throat. How did they miss us?"

"I don't know," Sharon said. "I'm just glad they did. They're huge."

As they walked into the classroom, JoJo said, "Get ready to draw your grasshopper."

"Might as well just get it done," Sharon said. "Mom said not to worry, just start."

"Hello, ladies," Mr. Markel called. "Sharon, are you ready to draw on the board for us?"

"Sure," she said, smiling.

"I have chalk right here," he said. Make it big. Cover this entire section of the board so people can see it in the back."

The girls set their books on their desks.

"Will you stand up there with me?" Sharon asked.

"Of course," JoJo said. "I'll hold the chalk for you."

JoJo watched as her new friend sketched the eyes and head of the grasshopper first, giving it a whimsical expression. JoJo smiled.

"He's so cute," she whispered. Sharon smiled at her and winked.

The back was next, and the wings, followed by the body, the grasping front legs, middle legs and huge back legs, powerful for jumping.

"Nice," Mr. Markel said. "Good job."

The girls walked to their seats, smiling, while Mr. Markel passed out grasshopper part identification diagrams and started class discussion.

"Sharon demonstrated for us that drawing a decent grasshopper can be done, quickly and well, I might add," he said. "By the way, Sharon, were you the one who drew grasshoppers all around the elementary school?"

She laughed, nodded.

"The little kids loved them," Mr. Markel said. "My son goes there. He rode his bike by and told me all about it. This morning there were dozens of little kids looking at your grasshoppers and hopping to school.

"Anyway, grasshoppers... Try to work with your specimens carefully. We need to examine them intact, and as we dissect them, we need to do each action carefully so as not to disturb the rest of the bodily organs and parts..."

When Mr. Markel finished the lesson, the class returned to their lab tables and specimens.

"The more I look at it, the more I notice what I didn't see before," JoJo said.

"That's true of anything you draw," Sharon said. "If I draw something once, I see the basics of it. If I draw something 10 times, the details become clearer and I notice more."

"Did that happen while you were drawing grasshoppers outside?"

"Yes, plus I got faster," Sharon answered. She looked at the teacher as he walked by. "Mr. Markel, can we put it on a microscope or something?"

"Maybe after it's dissected more," he said. "Use your magnifying glass for now. But you're right. There are parts that are fascinating under a microscope. We'll get into that later. Start with the big picture for now."

"Do you like science?" JoJo asked.

"Yes, always have," said Sharon. "When I was little I had a teacher who loved science, so I decided I love science, too. Most of us did. She made it fun. I get those kinds of books from the library because the deeper I get, the more interesting it becomes. I love to study deep."

"Here's the magnifying glass," JoJo said. "What are those pokey things on its back legs?"

"I don't know," Sharon said. "Are they in the book?"

"They're in the picture, but not named," JoJo said. "Mr. Markel, what are the pokey things on the back legs?"

"Can anyone tell us?" Mr. Markel asked. "Who can find the answer the fastest?"

All at once search engines on cellphones and tablets pulled up facts about grasshoppers as students dug for information.

"This class flew by," JoJo said, as they filed out the door at the end of the period.

"Good work," Mr. Markel called after them.

When JoJo opened her locker and placed her books and notebooks inside, she felt like something was wrong there. Then she realized it.

"My lunch is missing," she said. She looked under her jacket, no lunch.

"Sharon, did I leave my lunch on the floor or something?" she asked.

"Didn't you put it in your locker?" Sharon asked.

"I thought so, but it isn't here now," JoJo said. She felt in her inner jacket pocket for a small change purse with spare lunch money, and it, also, was gone.

"You go ahead to the lunch room," JoJo said. "I'll go ask Mrs. Stacey if I left my lunch in the car. I don't think I did. Anyway, I need a teacher's permission to go out to the parking lot to look."

"Okay," Sharon said. "see you in a little while."

After JoJo spoke with Mrs. Stacey and looked in the car, she did not find her lunch. Mrs. Stacey handed her enough money to buy her lunch in the cafeteria, and JoJo raced there just in time before the end of the line finished going through.

"I'm so grateful," JoJo said.

*Oh, no.* JoJo thought. *I can't carry the tray very well.*

Just then Sharon walked up beside her.

"Does Amanda's mom make cardamom cookies, too?" Sharon asked. "She seems to have some."

JoJo turned to look, and Amanda was talking to her friends, laughing and eating a sandwich. A note card, like the ones JoJo's mother uses, was on the table in front of Amanda, along with a protein drink and a juice pouch.

JoJo ran from the line and grabbed the note from the table. It was her mother's note, and JoJo's lunch. She looked at Amanda, kept the note and returned to her place in line to finish getting the school lunch.

"What's the matter?" the lunch lady asked kindly.

"Amanda stole my lunch today," JoJo said, "and the note from my mother."

The lunch lady turned and called over the supervisor. But when JoJo turned around, Amanda had gone. The remainder of JoJo's lunch was still at the table.

"I don't have much time to eat," JoJo said. "I'll tell the principal during seventh period when I have study hall."

The other girls in Amanda's group also left the room, leaving the remainder of JoJo's lunch the only thing left on the table.

JoJo read her mother's encouraging note, and tucked it into her pocket. After JoJo ate the school lunch and carried the empty tray to the cooks, she walked over to the table, picked up the unopened protein drink and juice pouch, and threw the rest away in the trash.

"Sharon, I"m sorry I wasn't much fun at lunch today," JoJo said.

"I don't blame you," Sharon said.

"I guess I am going to tell the principal after all," JoJo confided.

# 51

# SHE SAID, SHE SAID

Make time for people.

JoJo decided not to drink her protein shake or juice until after she spoke with Mr. Ferres. She and Sharon had to hurry to make it to North American history on time. But that class, also, resulted in lively discussion that made it interesting.

While Sharon went to art for seventh period, JoJo placed her books at her spot on the table in study hall, and asked the monitor if she could go to the principal's office. She received a hall pass, and walked to the office, preparing what she should say on the way.

*Dear God,* JoJo prayed silently, *please give me the right words. You love me and Amanda, so I'm praying for us both. Please help.*

When JoJo arrived at the office, the principal had his door closed with someone inside, the secretary said. JoJo left her name and a request to speak with Mr. Ferres, and that she was in study hall seventh period. She walked back to her seat and flipped open her algebra book to finish as many problems as possible in the remaining time of the period.

About 20 minutes later, JoJo heard her name over the intercom, calling her to the office. She decided to take her books with her.

Minutes later seated in front of Mr. Ferres, JoJo recounted the events. Amanda and the two girls trying to get her locker open, her change purse missing from her jacket pocket, and a description of the purse, Amanda's eating JoJo's sandwich with the contents of her lunch bag spread out on the table in front of her, including JoJo's mother's note, and Amanda's running out of the room as soon as she was found out.

Mr. Ferres listened, scribbled some notes, and listened some more.

"Would you happen to know anything about a hit list?" Mr. Ferres said.

"No," JoJo answered. She felt startled.

*What is going on?* JoJo thought. *God help!*

"Another student said you have a hit list in your locker with students' names on it," Mr. Ferres said sternly.

"No, I don't," JoJo insisted.

"Is it okay if I look?" Mr. Ferres asked.

"Sure," JoJo said, feeling confused and panicky. "But I don't have a hit list. I'm not that type of person."

"But you say three girls were trying to get your locker open this morning when you arrived at school today?"

"Yes. Amanda and two of her friends. I don't know their names," JoJo said.

"Did you report it?" he asked.

"I told Sharon, my friend who helps me carry my books," JoJo said. "But since they didn't get my locker open, and Amanda said she had the wrong locker and they walked away, I didn't tell any adults except Mrs. Stacey when I was looking for my lunch, before I went to the lunch room. Mrs. Stacey gave me lunch money for today."

"Okay. I'll talk to Sharon and Mrs. Stacey," Mr. Ferres said. His expression never changed during the entire conversation. JoJo wondered how she could be considered a suspect when her lunch was stolen.

Mr. Ferres sat silently looking at JoJo. She waited, not filling in the silence, and not squirming under his gaze.

"Let's go look in your locker," Mr. Ferres said.

They walked into the hallway and JoJo showed him her locker. She worked the combination, and as she opened the door, a piece of paper fluttered to the floor. Mr. Ferres picked it up by a corner. He showed it to JoJo, and she saw a list of names written on the paper, but most of the names she did not know.

"That's not my handwriting," JoJo said. "And I don't even know most of those people."

As they stood at the locker, one of Amanda's friends walked by and smirked at JoJo behind Mr. Ferres's back. JoJo just stood tall.

*God, you know who did this,* JoJo prayed. *I'm trusting you to get me out of it.*

"Which ones do you know?" Mr. Ferres asked.

"Well, I only know first names of Herman and Amanda. I didn't know their last names until now," JoJo said. "I don't know the other names, other than Sharon, and she's my friend who helps me. This doesn't make sense."

"Let's go back to the office," Mr. Ferres said. "But first, you said the note is not in your handwriting. Do you have anything I could use as a handwriting sample?"

"Yes, sir," JoJo said, pulling out a notebook. "Do you want a page of notes from the beginning of the year?"

"That will work," he said. "Let's talk this over in my office."

By the time they returned to the office, his expression changed.

"JoJo," Mr. Ferres said, "I believe you. Your handwriting and the handwriting on the list don't match. You did not know about the list, and you don't know the names. That doesn't make sense. I still have to report this to police. And you will have to answer their questions. In the meantime, does this look familiar?"

"It does. That looks like my change purse."

"It was found in a wastebasket in the restroom by a janitor," Mr. Ferres said.

"I haven't used the restroom yet today," JoJo said.

"I'm going to keep this until the police are finished with the case," Mr. Ferres said. "They're on their way. I need you to stay here until they are finished."

In a few minutes, a man in a crisp white shirt and dark blue tie arrived. His shoes were polished to a gleaming shine, and his dress slacks hit the top of his shoes at precisely the correct length. JoJo said nothing as she looked up into his blue eyes and noticed his meticulously cut and groomed light brown hair.

"I'll be going down the hall to talk to a couple of people," Mr. Ferres said. "You may interview JoJo here. She's the accused."

*The accused,* JoJo thought. *For all this time those girls have been playing dirty tricks on me, and now I'm the accused. God, I'm scared. And this isn't fair. And I don't know what to say or do."*

"Hi JoJo. I'm Capt. Randy," the man in the white shirt said, holding out his hand. JoJo shook it. "I'm a detective with the police department. We haven't met before, have we?"

"Um, no sir," she said.

"How are you doing today?" he asked.

"I thought I was doing okay until my lunch was stolen and this happened," JoJo said.

"What happened to your arm?" he asked.

"Well, that was last week," she said. "If you want to go back that far, this is going to be a long story."

"Let's do it," Capt. Randy said.

JoJo told him about the events leading up to when she and Mr. Ferres opened her locker.

"A paper fell out," JoJo said. "It doesn't make sense. If I had a list, why would it just fall out? And why are there names I don't know? And why isn't it in my handwriting? Not only that, but I'm not that type of person."

"What names do you know on the list?" Capt. Randy asked.

"Amanda, who stole my lunch today; Herman, who I'm supposed to be showing my marching band routine to so he can substitute for me this weekend, and Sharon, my friend who helps by carrying my books."

"I see," Capt. Randy said. "Do you know who accused you of having a list?"

"No," JoJo said. "But I think anyone could have put that in my locker. They don't even need the combination."

"UmmHmm," Capt. Randy said.

Mr. Ferres returned, and Capt. Randy asked if there were any writing samples.

"Yes," Mr. Ferres said. "This is a page of JoJo's notes from class this school year."

The detective compared the sample with the list.

"Any sample from Amanda?" Capt. Randy asked.

*Amanda accused me? After she stole my lunch? And I'm the accused?* JoJo felt furious inside, and she was thankful the two men were talking with each other and not paying attention to her at that moment.

"JoJo, where are your parents?" Capt. Randy asked.

"My mom is at work, and my dad died," she said quietly.

"I don't see a reason to take JoJo to the station," Capt. Randy said. "There are some things I'd like to check on. I just want to keep the girls separated."

"May I go to band?" JoJo asked. "Amanda is not in band."

"But Herman is in band," Capt. Randy said.

"Yeah, but he's helping me," JoJo said.

"See, that's what doesn't add up," Capt. Randy said to Mr. Ferres. "JoJo, I could drop you off at home. Can your mother meet us there? You need to be with an adult at all times, and that will keep you from having to go to the police station. I'd like to speak with your mother, too."

"I'll call her mother," Mr. Ferres said, leaving the room. He returned a few minutes later. "She will meet you at their house. This is the address. I did not tell her what this is about. I'll leave that up to you."

"Thank you," Capt. Randy said. "I'll get back with you after I speak with JoJo's mother."

"Right," Mr. Ferres said. "There are two others we need to speak with in the meantime."

"Are you ready, JoJo?" Capt. Randy asked.

"May I please go to my locker? I need my books and jacket," JoJo said. "I have homework to do. Plus, I have to give this back to Coach."

She unwrapped the bandage from her arm, but could not figure out how to wind it up one handed.

"I'll give it to the coach," Mr. Ferres said. "Which one?"

"I don't know his name," JoJo said. "Sharon knows which one. She got him to wrap my arm this morning. He wanted me to give the bandage to Herman after band."

"Okay, we'll get it to Coach," Mr. Ferres said. "Locker, yes? No?"

"I'm sorry, JoJo, we can't let you go to your locker right now," Capt. Randy said. "Let's get you home."

*I don't understand this,* JoJo thought. *I'm heartbroken. And this is embarrassing.*

# 52

# ANOTHER RIDE

Take out the garbage before it falls on the floor.

JoJo rode quietly in the back of the police car. She wasn't handcuffed, but at the moment she found it hard to be thankful for that fact.

*This is humiliating,* JoJo thought. *It was my lunch that was stolen, and my change purse that was stolen, and I didn't write that list.*

It was then that JoJo recalled a Bible story about a young man, Joseph, with a coat of many colors. His jealous brothers beat him up, took his coat and threw him in the bottom of a pit. Then they sold him to slave traders and told their father he was eaten by wild beasts. That was just the beginning of the story.

"Is this your house coming up?" Capt. Randy asked.

"Yes," said JoJo.

He turned into the driveway. A few minutes later, JoJo's mother arrived and parked her car next to the police car. JoJo saw a frantic look on her mother's face.

*Oh, no,* JoJo thought. *This is hurting my mom.*

Belinda held her hands out, palms turned upward.

"JoJo, what happened?" Belinda asked, seeming so upset JoJo didn't know what to say. They both looked at Capt. Randy.

"Can we go inside?" he asked.

"Sure," JoJo's mother said. They walked to the porch where she fumbled and dropped her keys, picked them up and stuck one key in the lock. JoJo saw her mother's hands shake.

*I'm so sad,* JoJo thought. *My mom doesn't deserve this either.*

Belinda opened the door and they walked inside. All three sat at the dining room table.

"Ma'am," Capt. Randy said. "I brought JoJo home to protect her, more than anything. Another girl said there was a hit list in JoJo's locker. The school looked, and there was a list, but JoJo didn't even know very many people on the list. Then we find out girls tried to get into her locker this morning, someone stole her lunch and JoJo found a girl eating it, with a note from you on the table in front of her. Come to find out, the girl eating the lunch was the same girl who accused JoJo. We have some more investigating to do. It was better for JoJo not to be at school for now. And I needed to leave her with an adult rather than take her to the station."

As Capt. Randy spoke, JoJo saw her mother relax somewhat. Still, she was called home from work.

*I can't believe things keep getting worse,* JoJo thought.

"Can JoJo go back to school tomorrow?" Belinda asked. "Or are we both to stay home? I don't have anyone to be with her and I need to work to provide for us. I can't afford to lose my job."

"I can appreciate that," Capt. Randy said. "I'll let you know as soon as I know more. Another detective is interviewing the other girl and her mother at the station."

"Thank you," Belinda said.

After Capt. Randy thanked them, said, "Good-bye," and left, JoJo and Belinda stood in the dining room and hugged each other.

"I was so scared," Belinda said.

"Me, too."

# 53

# PREVAILING WIND



Belinda listened as JoJo recounted the events of the day. She immediately opened her purse and took out the money to pay Alice back for JoJo's lunch.

After about two hours, the phone rang.

"Yes, this is Belinda Ward." She listened, and JoJo wished she would put it on speaker phone. "Okay, will do. Thank you for your call."

She hung up the phone and looked at JoJo.

"The school and police agreed you are allowed to return to school," she said. "I don't know what happened, but they're keeping the other girl, at least overnight."

"Mom, I don't feel safe," JoJo said. "If she comes back to school tomorrow, I don't feel safe. Can I stay home?"

An officer will be at the school tomorrow for an assembly," Belinda said. "They think you will be fine."

"Okay," JoJo said. "I'll trust you and God."

"This has been such a crazy day," Belinda said. "My boss called me in for a meeting this morning, and gave me a raise of $2 an hour and thanked me for being such a good worker. He said he didn't realize until the day you were hurt that I was providing for the family. Plus, when the school called, he was the one to answer the phone before he left town. He told me to go quickly, and not to worry because what he said this morning still stands."

"Wow. That's amazing," JoJo said. "There are good people in the world."

"Yes," Belinda agreed, "and we're going to keep finding more and more of them."

# 54

# UNSEEN RESULTS

*A life lived well is worth it.*

Even though JoJo only had her algebra book at home with her, Belinda insisted on driving her to school.

"Now take that money right back to Alice first thing this morning," she said. "And be sure to give her my note. I'm so thankful you didn't have to go hungry yesterday."

"Me, too," JoJo said. "Thanks, Mom. Love you."

"Love you, too, Baby Doll," Belinda said.

*I wish I could climb back in the car and go anywhere except school.*

But as her mother drove away, JoJo walked into the building and straight to Mrs. Stacey's room. They hugged and JoJo gave her a brief explanation. Mrs. Stacey seemed troubled.

"I'm sorry," JoJo said. "I didn't mean to upset you."

"You didn't, JoJo," Mrs. Stacey said. "But the information is helpful. I'm going to take it straight to the throne room of heaven."

JoJo walked up the hallway, not wanting to round the corner to go to her locker. But when she did, a police officer was standing where Amanda's group usually gathers. None of them were there.

*I'm so relieved,* JoJo thought. *Maybe today will be okay after all.*

The police officer greeted all of the students as they arrived, and shook hands with some of them. The football players seemed to be friends with him.

"Hey, where did you go yesterday?" Herman asked JoJo. "You left me hanging."

"That could not be helped," JoJo said, embarrassed and not wanting to even remember the day before, much less talk about it. She was glad when Sharon walked up to her, too.

"I'm allowed to help carry your books, but I'm not allowed to talk to you about yesterday or anything," Sharon whispered to JoJo.

"Okay," JoJo said, "But why not?"

"I told them what Amanda did to me at the other school," Sharon said. "That's why you're allowed to be here today."

"Thank you," JoJo said. "I wasn't allowed to take my books home last night. I don't have all of my homework done."

"Let's go in now," Sharon said. "The more you can get done before class, the less will be marked off. So at least it won't be so, so bad."

"You're right," JoJo said. "If I can't have an A, a B or C is still better than an F."

JoJo sat at her desk in the North American literature room and wrote furiously. Before the rest of the class arrived, she had written a page and a half of an essay, and stretched it to two pages before Mrs. Smith called for the papers to be turned in. JoJo scribbled a cover page with her name, class, date and section number, and handed in the essay with the others.

*I didn't get to proofread it,* she thought. *I wonder what regrettable mistakes there are in it. I can't worry about it. There's still too much to do.*

Biology homework included questions at the end of the chapter, and a multiple choice handout on the life cycle of grasshoppers.

*Just dig in and finish as much as possible,* JoJo thought. Once she started, the questions were not as hard as they first seemed.

The algebra homework was completed, but after the class checked the work, the teacher did not collect it.

After algebra, JoJo needed to use the restroom, so Sharon carried her books to biology and JoJo hurried into a stall. When she came out to wash her hands, there sat Amanda, slumping against the far wall under a window. The sight startled JoJo. Amanda's hair was disheveled and hanging over her red, tear-streaked face. She held a big knife to her bare forearm.

JoJo stopped, started to turn toward the door, then turned back toward the distraught girl, her enemy, the one she had been praying to God for.

"Whoa, Amanda," JoJo said. "What are you doing?"

"What does it look like?" Amanda growled, glaring at her.

JoJo didn't know what to say. Her heart was pounding.

*God help,* she prayed silently, desperately. *What should I say to her?*

"Amanda, don't," JoJo said, as a feeling of calm came over her. "Don't do it. Don't hurt yourself. You don't really want to, and we can figure this out. I don't know how, yet. But you can get through this, and things can get better. I know they can. Don't do anything right now while you're upset."

"What do you know about upset?" Amanda hissed. "I don't need you telling me what to do. You're the cause of this."

*Me? God, what happened? God, help!*

"Um, what did I do?" JoJo asked, not wanting to provoke Amanda, but hoping for a clue, for an out. "What are you talking about?"

"Yesterday, how come you didn't get into trouble?" Amanda said accusingly.

"Not get into trouble! What do you call getting called into the principal's office and getting a ride home in a police car?" JoJo countered. "And I didn't do anything."

"Oh, yes you did," Amanda sneered.

"Okay, what? What did I do wrong to anyone?" JoJo challenged.

"You took my boyfriend," Amanda practically spit the words at JoJo.

"Oh, no I didn't. I don't have a boyfriend, let alone take yours," JoJo said. "I've never even been on a date. So I don't know where you got your information, but it's wrong."

"Herman Heim."

"Herman?" JoJo responded. "What about Herman? He's not my boyfriend. Not only that, but I've never seen you with Herman."

"You took Herman. He was supposed to be my boyfriend. We were together all summer," Amanda said. "Then you show up and we're not together any more."

"He must have another flame, because Herman and I are not an item, and we never have been," JoJo said steadily.

"Not an item?"

"Nope."

"Then why is he always talking to you?"

"He doesn't, really, just little stuff," JoJo said. "I don't even know much about him."

"He's marching for you in the band," Amanda sneered.

"I didn't set that up," JoJo said. "I didn't even know Herman played trumpet until yesterday. That was set up by the band director and the coach."

"You didn't?"

"Nope," JoJo said. "Now put that thing down."

Amanda had a faraway look on her face, and she did not respond for a few minutes.

JoJo could feel her heart beating so fast it felt like it would jump out of her chest. But no words came to her, so she stood there, saying nothing.

*God, what do I say next?*

Amanda broke the silence.

"I went to my aunt's house, and there on the table was a beautiful present," Amanda said. "So I said, 'A present for me?' I went over to it and saw the pretty paper, and the purple bow. I love purple. 'My aunt bought me a present,' I said. So I picked it up and looked at the tag. It had your name on it. She's my aunt not yours. Why did she buy you a present, after all you've done to me? So I opened it, and inside a pretty box was a Bible, with 'JoJo' written in fancy gold letters on the front of it. So I took it out and ripped it up and threw it in the woods. She's my aunt, not yours."

"I forgive you," JoJo said quietly, barely able to be heard.

"What?" Amanda said. "I couldn't hear that."

"I forgive you," JoJo said. "All this time I've tried to be your friend, but you're mean to me. Now maybe I see why, a little bit. I forgive you. And God loves you. I've been praying for God to bless you."

"I don't believe in God," Amanda spat.

"I believe God for you. I pray for you. You could have a great life ahead of you," JoJo said. "But your way isn't working. We can work through all of this. There is a way through this. You don't need to hurt yourself. Put it down and slide it away, then let's figure this out. There is hope."

Amanda brushed the hair out of her face with the hand that wasn't holding the knife. JoJo waited.

"Why would you help me?" Amanda countered.

"I've tried to be a friend to you ever since I came here," JoJo said, noticing her own voice grow calmer.

Amanda dropped the knife a couple of inches away from her arm.

"Anyway, you can choose whatever friends you want," JoJo said, "even if you don't want to be friends with me. There are people who will help you. There is hope. All of these problems we face in school are temporary. Boyfriends are temporary. You don't have to be my friend if you don't want to. But there are people who care about you."

Suddenly two younger girls walked into the bathroom, looked and saw Amanda with the knife and froze, staring at her.

"Go get a teacher, or the principal," JoJo said. The girls ran out and told people in the hall about the knife.

Amanda didn't seem to be listening to them.

"You said people care?" she asked.

"I know people care," JoJo said. "People will get you good help. There is hope. Put that thing down and kick it over here, and let's get you some help."

To JoJo's surprise, Amanda slowly opened her hand and dropped the knife. It clattered to the floor as George ran into the bathroom doorway. JoJo held up her hand for him to stop. The police officer ran up behind him.

"Kick it away from you," JoJo said. "Help is here. There is hope."

Amanda kicked the knife and it skidded to the doorway. Mr. Ferres also ran up to the men.

"Don't touch it with your hands," the police officer warned. "Come on, Amanda. She's right. There is hope. Let's get you some help."

George and Mr. Ferres helped Amanda stand up and held her as they walked out of the bathroom and into the office. The police officer checked JoJo, asking if she were injured. Then he picked up the knife carefully in a white cloth like a handkerchief.

"Are you JoJo?" he asked. She nodded. "Would you tell me what happened?"

JoJo described the incident, which seemed like it took hours.

"I found out what God can do with a tiny prayer," she said. "I'm just glad I went to the bathroom before I saw her sitting there. That was so scary I hope I never have to go through anything like that again."

"You're right. Kids shouldn't have to go through anything like this," the officer said. "Thank you for talking her through it. Most people who say they're going to hurt themselves, don't really want to. They want another way out, but they're so upset they can't see it."

JoJo walked to the principal's office with the police officer, so she could write out a statement about the incident. Capt. Randy was standing there, too.

"Apparently Amanda ran away from her mother today," Capt. Randy said. "We've been looking for her for two hours. We don't even know how she got into the school, unless she arrived before we notified people.

"How did you do it? I'm trained in crisis negotiations," Capt. Randy said. "But how did you know what to say?"

"I didn't. She was so upset," JoJo said. "It looked impossible, and I just wanted to forget about washing my hands and walk out the door. But something inside stopped me.

"I looked at her," JoJo said. "She looked so hopeless and scared. I prayed, 'God help!' And just started talking. I don't know why, but I wasn't afraid for me. She was trying to hurt herself. I just knew.

"She thought I took her boyfriend, and I didn't," JoJo said. "So I prayed for help again, and something changed. I told her there is hope and there are people who care, and we would get her help. Will you please get her good help?"

JoJo looked at Capt. Randy and paused.

As JoJo was speaking, Alice Stacey walked into the office. She came alongside and hugged JoJo gently, so as not to hurt her sore arm.

"I just heard a little bit about what happened," Mrs. Stacey said. "The principal called me on my room phone. Thank you so much, JoJo. I've been so worried about both of you. Just 20 minutes ago, I felt a need to pray for you, so I did."

"You know the sermon on Sunday?" JoJo asked. "Pastor Don said four things: Love, pray, do good and bless. I've been praying since then. Love, not until now. Do good, still needs to be done. Bless, I tried to speak hope. And I learned God can take a tiny prayer and turn it into something huge."

Alice looked at her for a few moments.

"Yes, this is huge," Alice said. "Amanda is my niece. Her late father was my brother. And I know she hasn't treated you right. But I'm so thankful for what you did today. You did good and I'm so thankful. Yes, we are going to get Amanda some good help.

"Do you know what her name means?" Alice asked. JoJo shook her head. "Worthy to be loved by God. My brother named her before he died."

Alice knocked at Mr. Ferres's door, and the men inside asked her to come in.

*Maybe Amanda and I do have something in common,* JoJo thought. *She lost her dad, too.*

Mr. Ferres came out of his office, gave JoJo a sheet of white paper on a clipboard, and asked her to write a statement for the police about what happened. For a moment her mind went blank.

*I can't remember,* she thought. *It all happened so fast.* So she sat down and scribbled on a lower corner of the paper with the pen. Then step by step, JoJo wrote what happened in the girls bathroom.

When JoJo turned in the paper to Mr. Ferres, he thanked her.

"Are you sure you're okay?" he asked. "This was a pretty big deal today."

"I'm sure," JoJo said. "I serve a great big God, and he's awesome. May I please have a pass to get into biology class?"

"You surely may," Mr. Ferres said. He wrote, "Please admit this heroic young lady into biology class! Mr. Elvin G. Ferres, principal."

"Thank you," JoJo said. She smiled at him and walked out of the office to class.

When JoJo handed the pass to Mr. Markel, he read it, then read it aloud to the class. They all turned and looked at JoJo.

"What happened?" Mr. Markel asked her. Everyone looked at her expectantly.

"It's a very long story," JoJo said, smiling and a little embarrassed. "We don't have time for it right now. Besides, I"m not allowed to tell yet."

"Okay, back to grasshoppers," Mr. Markel called out. The class groaned.

Sharon looked at JoJo as she walked to her seat.

"What happened?" she whispered. "I was so worried about you."

"You wouldn't believe it," JoJo answered. "All I can say right now is: I can't wait until my arm gets better. I need to build a kite."

# JoJo's Cardamom Cookies

JoJo's Cardamom Cookies

Mom says: Place egg and butter or margarine on counter to warm up a little bit and to soften, so mixing will be easier.

Start with two bowls. Place dry ingredients except sugar in one bowl, mix well.

Dry ingredients:

1 3/4 Cup of all-purpose flour

1/2 teaspoon of ground cardamom

1/2 teaspoon of ground cinnamon

1/4 teaspoon of salt

Ingredients for mixing bowl:

1/2 Cup of butter or margarine, softened

3/4 Cup of packed brown sugar

1 egg

1/2 teaspoon vanilla

Place softened (but not runny) butter or margarine in a mixer bowl with the brown sugar and beat it until it's fluffy. Add the egg (not the shell) and vanilla and beat them together very well.

**209**

Then stir in the dry ingredients a little at a time, just with a spoon until it's mixed together well.

Cover the mixer bowl with plastic wrap, a lid that fits on it or a plate and set it inside the refrigerator for two hours so the dough is easier to shape.

Mom says: Before you shape the dough into balls, check the oven to make sure nothing is in there. After the dough chills when you start to shape it into balls, turn on the oven to 350 degrees. It takes awhile for an oven to heat up to the right temperature.

Mom says: grease the cookie sheets with shortening so the cookies don't stick to them. The shortening should be on there evenly, not in a globby mess.

Shape the cookies into the size of a large jawbreaker or gumball Try to make them all the same size so they will bake evenly

Place cookies on the cookie sheet about two inches apart. Place a small amount of flour on a saucer. Find a glass with a smooth bottom, and dip the glass in the flour. Then press down on a cookie until it is flat but not too thin. Repeat with all of the cookies.

Mom says: In olden days, women made these cookies look fancy by flattening them with a cookie press that had a pattern carved into it. But if you don't have a cookie press, you can still enjoy the cookies by flattening them with a glass or clean jam jar.

Bake a pan of cookies for 8 minutes at 350 degrees.

Mom says: It's really important to set a timer either in the kitchen or on your cell phone so you bake these cookies for just eight minutes. Pay attention. Place pot holders on the counter or table to set the hot pan down.

Place the second pan in the oven. Set the timer for 8 minutes. Then transfer the hot cookies to a cookie rack to cool. This recipe makes about 70 small cookies. If you make the balls bigger, there will be fewer cookies and they might not bake as well.

Mom says: If this is your first time trying this cookie recipe, then test your oven by baking just one cookie for 8 minutes to see if that is how you like it. If you want a crisper cookie, add a minute to the baking time.

JoJo says: These cookies taste great with a cup of tea or a glass of milk!

Love,

Dad

# LET'S TALK

1. When you first meet someone, what do you know about that person? What does that person know about you?
2. What does it feel like to be the new person in a group, or at a school, a church or a workplace?
3. What does the Bible say about how to live at peace with everyone, as far as it depends on you? Write these passages down and memorize them.
4. Does this story provide ideas about good ways to interact with others?
5. Does this story show bad examples of ways people interact with others?
6. Does the Bible show good ways to act as well as bad ways to act? Should people copy the bad examples in the Bible just because they're in the Bible? Or did God want us to avoid making the same mistakes?
7. How can talking ahead of time about "a bad idea set in motion" lead to better outcomes?
8. What happens when a person prays for enemies who mistreat them?
9. Who is the only perfect person who ever lived?
10. How can God love people when each of us does so many wrong things every day?

11. Who do you know who has experience, knowledge and good judgment?
12. How are we changed by spending time each day reading the Bible and seeking God in prayer?
13. How much does God love you?
14. Do bad things happen to people who try to live a good life?
15. What is the benefit of living life God's way rather than screaming, fighting and kicking for our own way?
16. Have you ever said or done anything that hurt someone else? Did you mend the relationship God's way? If not, what would happen if you did?
17. What does creating a mutually respectful relationship look like?
18. When law enforcement officers show up at a door, usually people are upset for whatever reason. Officers are trained to deescalate the situation by speaking slower and in a lower volume. Have you ever tried this?
19. Think about your relationship with your best friend. Why does that relationship work well?
20. What does the Bible say about forgiveness?
21. Have you ever heard, "No bad deed goes unpunished?" In the Bible, who punishes bad deeds?
22. How do you feel about the relationship between JoJo and Belinda? JoJo and her dad?
23. What is your favorite dad quote in the book?
24. Do you think JoJo and Belinda maintain a strong relationship? Why or why not?
25. Is there anything you want to do differently after reading this book?

# ACCEPT GOD'S GIFT

Dear sweet JoJo,

If only we could be perfect and never do anything wrong, ever. But we can't. Each person does wrong things. That includes me, your mom and you. So don't be surprised if you see flaws in yourself and other people. They're there as part of being human. The good news is God loves each of us, anyway.

Jesus is God's son who came to earth to make a way for us to live forever with him in Heaven. Jesus suffered what each of us deserve, because he loves us that much. Wow!

Why do we deserve to suffer? Because every person on the planet is selfish and God hates selfishness.

The Bible calls selfishness, "sin." In many ways we sin and do wrong against others and against God. The penalty for sin is death. Jesus died for us, to satisfy our sin debt. Then Jesus rose from the grave three days later.

Since God is perfect, he cannot allow sin in his presence in Heaven. Jesus volunteered to be a bridge for us, so we can go to Heaven, too. Jesus provided the only way people can go to Heaven.

The way to accept God's gift to you, is to talk to him and tell him you know you sin and do wrong things, and you don't want to sin any more. Ask God to forgive you, not because you deserve forgiveness, but because Jesus paid your penalty by shedding his blood on the cross. Ask Jesus to be your Savior and your Lord meaning he is the one who guides your life now. Walking with Jesus is an amazing adventure!

Write down the date. This day is your spiritual birthday when you are born again by the Holy Spirit. Tell your mom.

Walking with Jesus isn't easy. Some people won't understand. But stand in; don't shrink back. Jesus is worthy of your honor and allegiance.

Love forever,
Dad

# WISDOM FOR A TOUGH TIME

Think before you act.

If you are thinking about hurting yourself or others, DON'T DO IT!

Get help right now.

You may feel justifiably awful, but emotions come and go.

You may be going through your worst nightmare, but problems are temporary.

A mountain of obstacles may be towering over you, but circumstances can change.

With the right help, you can walk through the horrible situation and come out better and stronger on the other side.

How do you find good help? Do all of these and don't give up hope:

1. Pray and ask God for good help and for his guidance to the right people.
2. Read the Bible to find information on the topic of your struggles.
3. What wise adults do you know? Seek them for advice and follow through on good ideas.

4.    Talk to a pastor, who probably is trained in the Bible, but not necessarily trained in counseling. Ask the pastor for a reference to a Christian counselor.

5.    Counselors have different specialties, for example, self harm or domestic violence or sexual assault. Find a counselor who understands your type of situation.

6.    If the person or persons you go to can't help, keep looking until you find someone who can help you. That person is out there. Have hope. Keep praying. Trust God.

7.    If you are in danger and need emergency help, call the emergency number for the first responder, police and fire departments in your area.

8.    The 988 Suicide Prevention Hotline accepts calls, texts and chats. Dial 988. If you don't know what to say, it's okay. Reach out for help anyway.

**Violet Barkley**
*Wilhelm Photography*

Love for Jesus, care for the hurting and a heart for encouraging teens led Christian author Violet Barkley to tell stories as a way to inspire young people.

Violet Barkley developed digital-first journalism skills while covering schools, governments and first responders in northern Ohio.

A mother of four grown children, Violet Barkley is a grandmother of three.

The Wise and Strong series is used best as a discussion tool between teens and adults who care for them. It is recommended for adults to read and discuss the books in groups of other adults to think through social issues prayerfully together. Any young person can walk in on a bad idea in motion, and each needs positive ideas for handling situations in a Christian way.

www.ingramcontent.com/pod-product-compliance
Lightning Source LLC
Chambersburg PA
CBHW011430310726
48972CB00011B/2996